The Gaudy Place

Also by Fred Chappell

IT IS TIME, LORD

THE INKLING

DAGON

THE WORLD BETWEEN THE EYES

The Gaudy Place

FRED CHAPPELL

Harcourt Brace Jovanovich, Inc., New York

The epigraph is from the play "Purgatory" in the *Collected Plays* of
William Butler Yeats. Copyright 1934, 1952 by The Macmillan Company.

Dedicated to Carolyn Kizer
and to Arthur Dixon
and to the memory of Mrs. F. B. Davis

What's right and wrong?
My grand-dad got the girl and the money.

—W. B. YEATS

The Gaudy Place

Arkie

Consider Arkie.

(But it breaks your heart.)

Teacher used to tell him he didn't exist.

Arkie shook his head angrily. "Yes I do. I do that." Immediately belligerent. He wasn't sure what it meant, *to exist,* but he knew that whatever it was it was no good for Arkie. Some sort of con, he bet. Arkie would bet you.

"You got a driver's license?"

"No."

"You got a social security number?"

"No."

"Birth certificate?"

"I don't know. Maybe I got that."

Teacher grinned. "And no school records and no vaccination scars and no doctor's records and no dentist's records. I guess you don't even have a mailing address."

"I got places I can get letters."

"How do you know? You never got any letters. You can't be sure, can't be sure of anything." He still grinned that skinny grin. He got a Herbert Tareyton between thin trembling fingers and took a long time getting it lit. "Don't you see?" He coughed:

sound like metal scraping metal. "Officially you don't even exist. Nothing proves it."

In a desultory voice: "I do though." Arkie was bored now.

"Have you got a real name?"

"James Parker McClellan."

"Not that anybody ever uses it. And how old are you?"

"Sixteen."

"*Horse*shit. You can tell the cops that when they come around checking. You're fourteen years old. Fifteen, maybe. You wouldn't know which yourself."

"Gimme a stab."

"Maybe in a minute I will." He propped his chin on a shaky hand. "What's your mother and father's name?"

Arkie shrugged and went away, leaving Teach sitting at the bar. Teacher was a fat waste of time always. This was in the Ace and ten-thirty in the morning and there was nothing moving, nothing, or Arkie wouldn't have spent this long with him. All the time he'd known Teacher he'd never got a thing out of him, not a penny. Teacher was 0, absolute. Not a teacher anyhow. Everybody called him that because he always wore this grimy corduroy jacket, color of dago red, with cigarette burns in unlikely spots. The jacket had wide side pockets, and always in one of the pockets was a paperback book, a gangster or a fuck or a cowboy. Teach sat in the bars and read the books until he got too blind drunk to see the pages. But talk. He'd talk. Jesus God, he'd cave your ears in.

He looked into the other room, the bigger room with the dance floor, but nothing was happening. A tall guy with an open white shirt and a dirty apron was bending over a mop bucket. Arkie could smell the bitter disinfectant even from where he stood.

"Hey John, you seen Clemmie?"

The big fellow looked up without straightening his body. He had a wide face, white as sugar. "Not since last night I ain't. She ain't been in this morning yet."

When he went back through the other room Teacher had al-

4

ready planked open a book and was staring at it, leaning his head on his left hand. Arkie made out not to look at him, silly bastard. He went out the door into the cool sunlight of early May. He had to shield his eyes, glancing across the street a few doors up and down. Juanita's Place didn't look any more lively than the Ace, the whole scene was a cold deck. This was the very worst time of day, with the hardasses at their nine-to-fives and the pigs still laying up. Most Arkie could hope for was to run into some hungover gungho who still had a few bucks and maybe juice him for a couple of quarters. If he was woozy enough. More likely all he could get was a cold drink here and there off the bread men or beer men or meat men on their daily rounds. He hated these hours, nothing moving, and the joints not really wanting anything to move yet, trying to get last night's crud off the floors. Arkie never felt right until about two o'clock in the afternoon, when the bars closed their solid front doors and the air conditioning went on and the soft lights came up, the game machine lights and the juke lights. Just wait till he'd found his con and got a little dump laid by: you wouldn't see Arkie all day till the moon came out. . . . It was awful what a headache he got from sunlight.

He jingled the coins in his pocket, turned right abruptly and down Gimlet Street he went, listlessly jingling. Today he'd staked himself to seven bucks, feeling when he'd got up this morning that he was going to be lucky or unlucky, pretty big one way or the other. (He hoped to hell.) Seven, man, was a heavy one-third of what he had in the world. But with an hour's maneuvering he'd upped it by only fifteen cents, piling trash bottles out on the curb down at the Rebel Cafe. Gimlet Street ran up a steep slouched hill, and Arkie was going down, past remnant goods stores, secondhand furniture stores, past dingy newsstands, upholstery shops, sandwich factories. Three blocks down he turned right on Flint Street, starting uphill again. It was a hilly goddam town, Braceboro. Bunker County was a hilly goddam county. The whole western slab of North Carolina was nothing but rocks, briars and goddam hills. —But suppose he'd turned left coming out of the Ace. Four short blocks and he would have been standing in the Braceboro town square where he could have inspected a big green metal statue of a guy on a horse. Zebulon Johns, it said on the marble base of the statue. Patriot and Philanthropist. 1834–1906. Green Zeb, Arkie knew, was some kind of old-time gungho (holding a sword) and politician. Pieraker. All statues were of pierakers. . . . That's the kind of crazy apple this town was, rotten at the heart, but bright and shiny on the outside, jacketed with golf links and shopping centers.

He went into the Big Bunny. Squelch was behind the counter, a short red-haired bulgy man. His arms were folded, his big steel-rimmed shoe was propped up on the drink cooler.

"Squelch. Like you for a quarter."

No, he wouldn't move. Not a flicker.

"Come on."

You might as well talk to the fireplug.

"Come on, Squelch. A little action. Make it a dime, make it a dollar, If I ain't like you I rare up and holler."

Heavily he unfolded his arms and refolded them. Gave Arkie a clear bottle-green eye. "See you for five." Squelch had a soft voice, low, and it always sounded ominous.

"Christamighty."

He could almost take it. He could use the cash and he could ride the stolid barkeep for a month about losing it. If he won. But five bucks, no, man. Today was Friday and come Monday night old man Johnson was going to stomp up the stairs and gouge him seven bucks for that farthole he called a room. And if Arkie didn't have it he could just punch the t.s. card and head for citizensville. Sleep on the sidewalk with Dick Tracy and Orphan Annie tucked under his chin. . . . Well no, it really wasn't all that bad. If it gave plumb out, he could pile in with Clemmie or one of the other pigs, as long as they weren't jockeying a john. But what kind of life was that for a man?

"You know I can't go no five bucks. Bring it down to man-size." Arkie did his little dance. "If you fly too high, Then you sure gonna die."

6

Squelch spent a long time getting ready to talk. "Been a slow week, Arkie. Here it's Friday already. I ain't got time for no chickenshit bets with ever gutterpickins that comes dragging in."

"Ah hell." Dispirited, he straddled one of the short bar stools and twirled twice around. "Gimme a stab."

He took the Camel from Squelch and got it safely lit before he let the mild careful whine seep into his voice. "You got no call to cuss me like that, you know it? Gutterbaby or whatever you said."

Squelch shrugged.

"Hey." Now his voice was lively again, enthusiastic. "Did you get the line yet?"

"Not yet."

"What'll you give me to go and get it for you?"

"It ain't in yet."

"It'll come in in about an hour. I'll run and get it for a quarter."

"What for? You know Walker's just going to call it in here. The fuzz ain't hooked into his phone no more."

"What's the good of taking a chance like that? A quarter's the cheapest bail money you ever went."

"Let's just wait and see if he calls." He leaned slightly forward and began to sound confidential. "He'll know whether it's safe or not. He always knows how it stands. See? He's got to know. That's how he got where he is."

"Ah hell."

Day to day, minute to minute, vain hopes were what Arkie fed upon. Two months ago, Danny Walker, who received the out-of-state gambling odds on all the sports for the Braceboro bookmakers, had found out that his telephone was going to be tapped. Every day for two weeks Arkie had earned fifty cents a stop for bringing the line to Walker's customers. Harder work than you'd think, because Walker was jittery and wouldn't allow Arkie to write anything down. But he never forgot: "State and four; Villanova and eight; Florida State and two . . ." He could jabber it off like a radio announcer, faster than they could take it down, and never a mistake. He could carry policy numbers too, all in his head like that. Those had been rich days for Arkie; that was something else he hadn't forgot. And every now and then Walker would have another case of nerves and Arkie picked it up, but it was nothing solid, nothing regular.

"Ah hell." These were sour sad hours.

Squelch started picking his teeth.

"I'm on the move," Arkie said. "I'll see you later."

"Yeah," Squelch said. "I'm damn sure of that."

Big Bunny my ass. Big wad of nothing . . . And the harrying painful sunlight . . . Back on Gimlet he turned right again, still going downhill, edging into mule territory now. Here it looked more interesting, the traffic noisier, people talking, even a juke blaring away in one of the joints. But Arkie had the educated eye, knew it all already. There was nothing here but mules, standing around with their hands in the pockets of their bib overalls and mouthing at each other and spitting big resounding gobs of tobacco juice. They would squeeze a quarter or a dime till you could slide it under the nail of your pinkie. Mules were what Arkie called truck farmers. They parked their dented pickup trucks at the bottom of the hill, where Gimlet joined Rance Avenue, and sold their produce off the truck beds. Open-air market. They were all dumb bastards. Arkie wished that he was getting just a little piece of what they all had to pay in to Burn Ryan so they wouldn't get their produce slopped and trampled, not get their tires slashed. He shrugged tiredly. That wasn't for Arkie, that heavy stuff. He had just turned fourteen (according to his own cloudy reckoning) and he was little for his age.

(Not that you could tell from his face. He looked whatever age you thought he did.)

He wandered into the Lucky Star and spoke to the first guy he saw, a mule sitting at the bar with a cup of mud. He was the mule type perfect and complete. Dumb from hairline to clodmashers. Lean, freckled, sandy-haired; the faded bib overalls and a red sweatshirt gone gray under the armpits.

"Hey. Match you for the piccolo," Arkie said. Piccolo, that was mule talk for the juke.

The guy looked him over, up and down, and Arkie stood easy, carelessly smiling. This was where you had to move very slowly; nothing scared away quicker than a mule.

"What are you going to play, then?" The farmer had to consider this a canny question. You wouldn't catch him putting up a good hard-earned ten-cent piece for some kind of city trash music he couldn't stand to listen to.

"Ever what you like," Arkie said. "Bill Monroe. Mac Wiseman. Lester and Earl."

"Just for a dime?"

"For one thin dime."

Look at him. Tight bastard had already sold his rutabagas and his pockets were probably running over with dump. But spend more than a dime? Not till it snows green money out of the sky.

The guy fished a quarter out of his bib pocket. Arkie listened to the change rattle, a good double handful. Arkie made sure the mule saw him staring at the ceiling while he was shaking the coin in his loose fist; but he saw too that it was going to come heads. Arkie, man, he's got those sharp eyes. He pulled a dime from his pocket, turned it once and laid it on the counter.

The guy wouldn't uncover yet. Grinned at Arkie like he'd just sold him a bushel of rotten turnips at an outrageous price. "You're like me, that right?"

"You got it right," Arkie said. "I'm matching you." Patience, Lord, give us patience.

"Play that there piccolo, boy."

Arkie had put down tails.

"Well," he said, "I'm damn. You sure can't win em all." He picked up his dime and went back toward the juke. "What would you be wanting to hear?"

"They got 'Foggy Mountain Breakdown' on that music box?"

"They got it."

They had it always, they're going to have it on forever.

He punched the buttons and came back and sat on the stool

9

next to the farmer and ordered a Pepsi in a glass. "And could you give me cube ice in that, Bill?" He turned to the farmer. "Can't stand this mush ice in my cold drink," he said.

The mule was still pleased with himself; he hardly heard the fiddle and the banjo. "You can't win em all," he told Arkie. Still grinning like a jack-o'-lantern.

"That's the dying truth," agreed Arkie. He shook his head ruefully and got out one of his own loose cigarettes and lit it. He let the index finger of his right hand curl over the edge of the glass and rest gently on the ice cube floating in the soft drink. "You bring some truck into market this morning?"

"Yep."

"How's the market going?"

"Pretty good. Ought to get better."

"Who's watching your stuff for you now?"

"I reckon my brother is. Leastways, that's what I left him doing."

By now his finger felt cold enough to turn the trick and Arkie casually wiped the wetness from the finger on his pants leg. He really didn't care about the other chance; God knows, he didn't have the stomach to sit out in that sunlight this morning, nursing some dumb mule's rutabagas. Suddenly: "Hey. I bet you I can hold this cigarette longer than you can. Hold it like this, I mean." He held it lengthwise, the burning end pressed against his index finger. He made a horrible painful face and dropped the cigarette almost immediately.

When the guy started grinning again Arkie knew he had him. If there was one thing mules had confidence in it was their goddam callouses. "All right," he said. "How much you want to bet?"

"Dollar."

"Well, all right," he said. "You sure are one betting man."

"Can't help it," Arkie said. "I got it in my blood." He picked up the cigarette from where he had dropped it on the bar. "I'll go first." He held it between thumb and forefinger for thirty seconds. The mule watched him intently, but he didn't quiver a muscle, nothing showed in his face. Finally the live coal began to tingle through the coldness, and Arkie handed over the cigarette. "There you go," he said. "Thirty seconds by the wall clock."

The mule wasn't so dumb he thought he could do it, but he had to give it a try. He got seven seconds before he flung it down. "They's some kind of trick to that," he said resentfully.

"Ain't no trick. Just takes will power."

"Yeah? Let's see your hand."

Arkie showed him. Nothing to see.

"It's some kind of trick or other."

"No it ain't, I'm telling you. The secret is, you got to think about something else while you keep hold of it. The secret is, not to think about it." He drank down his Pepsi in two heavy swallows and rose. "Well, I be seeing you, old-timer. You take it easy now."

"Wait a minute." The farmer was pondering; he wanted at least a piece of his dollar back. "What say we match one more time for the piccolo?"

"I can't stay to listen," Arkie said. "I got to go and see a feller. But I'll match you for the dime."

"No; match for the piccolo. We'll go for a quarter this time."

"Well," Arkie said, "if you think it'll make you happy."

They matched.

"Well hell," the mule said. "This ain't my day. This ain't my day and that's the living truth."

"You can't win em all."

Arkie departed.

Stupid, Christamighty stooopid.

And with mules it took practically forever. Look how much time and money he'd spent just to juice one slow farmer. Half an hour it took to make the dollar, just jollying the guy along. And then you had to count out a dime for the bait, that first bet on the juke, and then another eleven cents for the cold drink. In half a day's hard scrabbling he'd come up with ninety-four cents, and

11

that was including the work he'd done with the trash bottles. A man could starve; buddy, you know it for true. Somewhere, Arkie was certain of it, somewhere there was a real fine con, not a big one, but a good solid one that it didn't take a lot of capital to get off the ground with. A good solid con he could work by himself. It had to be by himself; anybody you went in with was older and a lot bigger than you. So they paid you off in bottle caps and if you tried to mention anything they stomped your ass around the block. He was going to ask Clemmie to ask Oxie for him. That Oxie, everybody knew about him, and a lot of people said they knew him, but hardly anybody really did. Clemmie knew him: she was one of Oxie's whores. And Arkie knew Clemmie. That would be his in. And if anybody had a con up his sleeve it was Oxie. Smart. Hadn't he come off Gimlet Street and got away clean? He wished he already knew Oxie; he wished they were a.h. buddies; wished he could call him on the phone right now this minute.

Where now?

He was beginning to feel a little hungry but it was close on to the lunch hour already. The hour that was either too early or too late for Arkie. When people were eating Arkie wasn't welcome in the cafes or joints. Everybody was too busy, running around taking orders and frying and wiping the tables and counting up the dump. They didn't want Arkie around trying to juice the eaters, getting underfoot and balling up the timetable. And they didn't want to take the time out to get him his cheeseburger. (Well done, with mustard and lettuce and tomato. No onions: Arkie was continually meeting the public.) But after lunch it was time to start drinking again and then they didn't care what he did. Actually they rather liked having him about. Good for business, if you looked at it right. He upped the take on the pinball machines and the bowling machines, the jukes and the pool tables. He was always matching for drinks. He kept people joking and hollering and talking and drinking, with his poems and that little dance of his, and that was maybe the best thing he did. Because when the johns were talking and laughing they weren't fighting, busting up the windows and bar mirrors and furniture. All that was fine. But not at mealtimes.

(Arkie: he could be an annoying little prick too.)

It was getting along in the day and he still hadn't run into Clemmie. No telling what that meant, he just never knew. She might simply be laying up—she was lazy enough for two mauds her size—or she might be in the hospital with a busted jaw or lying in a muddy ditch somewhere with her throat ripped open. He shuddered. The mauds had it tough. He didn't like to think about it. Let's see: last night before she went off she had gouged him for a dollar. (So. He was more or less used to that from Clemmie.) He hadn't been able to place the john she had picked up; a stranger to Gimlet. He had looked all right, short, blue-eyed guy, pretty well dressed. But what did that mean? Not a goddam thing. By the time a maud found out that the john was crackers, had some weird hang-up and was going to slice her, it was far too late. He didn't like to think about it. Not that it was any skin off Arkie's ass, not really; but he kept thinking about Clemmie in lots of different ways. He felt that something might be going to pan out there.

He wandered through the truck market. The crowd was thinning out now, though the housewives kept driving up in their shiny cars, still for Godsake dressed in pajamas and housecoats. Hair in funny-looking curlers. What made them get out of the sack? If he had that kind of money . . . Parked at the curb was a brand-new dark green Buick with the windows down. The dame that owned it was across the street, probably stridently trying to screw a mule down on his rutabagas. Arkie could just picture her. The windows were down, but there were no keys in the ignition. Arkie wasn't thinking about stealing the car, just because he didn't know how to drive. (How could he have learned that?) But he knew where he could have peddled the keys for a couple of bucks. *Hyook.* He hawked up and spat on the back seat, on the dark gray new-smelling felt. They hadn't got the plastic on the upholstery yet.

Here among the mules the number of flies had increased. Arkie

13

rubbed his nose with his wrist, not caring for the smells of vegetables and jonquils and fresh earth. The sunlight seemed worse. When he cut the corner of Rance Avenue he was in the shadow of the buildings and he felt a lot better.

Up this hill and down, up this hill again.

If you went down Gimlet, then you had to climb Rance. . . . Arkie's universe was minuscule, actually comprising an area of about fourteen blocks, although he knew of course that there were other places he could go when he wasn't trying to gouge the dime, the quarter, the dollar. (When would that be?) But, you know, fourteen blocks is a pretty big territory, and this was the place where you could go not only round and round, you could also go up and down. On Gimlet Street you could go so far down you would never see daylight again. . . .

Now he had reached his goal, the Teeny Tavern. Every now and then he would hole up in here over the lunch hours. It was a little bitsy place, about twelve feet wide and twenty feet long, stuck between a rundown tailor's shop and the warehouse for a roofing firm; Arkie could use it because it was too small to serve meals. Nothing to eat in here but stale potato chips and pretzels and peanut butter crackers in the dusty jar. Drink your beer and get out. When Arkie entered the little white-haired man behind the counter didn't come to see what he was up to. He was deaf and nearsighted and mostly oblivious to what went on; he seemed to be going over again and again in his mind something that had happened to him a long time ago. A nervous tic kept jerking below his right eye and now and then his lips flinched, trembled, as if the little old man were trying to form a word that had never been spoken on this human earth, a single word that would cleanse, heal and transform. . . . Arkie had a notion about him: once upon a time, years and years ago, some maud had given him the screw and this old guy was still trying to figure out what had happened. This was the kind of con Arkie longed for: one that warped the mind, so that twenty years later you were still blinking your eyelids and wondering where it had gone wrong.

14

No machines in here, except for an old beat-up Silvertone radio that Arkie had never heard turned on. No action of any kind in here. Guzzle your suds and get your ass out. Arkie dragged a slat-bottomed chair away from a table and sat, tipping the chair back against the wall. He shifted and reshifted; folded his arms; crossed his legs. And then he dozed off, dreaming.

—What does Arkie dream about?

—O Lord, please, let's don't talk about it. It's too garish and disconnected and bewildering. The kind of fantastic jungle no sound man will ever set foot in.

—But when he dreams of Arkie, how does he see himself?

—Just the way you and I do. As taller and stronger and wiser and tougher than he is on Gimlet Street.

—Is that all?

—That's enough. It's more than enough.

In an hour or so he was awakened by voices, but he didn't open his eyes immediately. Arkie had learned after various unpleasantnesses that it was best to play possum after napping until he'd remembered exactly where he was. Oh yeah . . . The Teeny. . . . Nothing was going to bother him in here. A couple of drivers for the roofing company were taking a break, came in to snatch a beer before going back on the job. He rose gingerly and stretched, replaced his chair and went out. What time was it? And where, goddammit, was Clemmie? He slouched into Diamond Billiards and got a cold Pepsi from the machine. Wanted to wash the sleep-film out of his mouth; it made him feel greasy all over. Wandered to the back table to look at Johnny Wyzscysky practicing.

The skinny paste-faced young man glanced at him. "Here you go, Arkie. Bet you a quarter I can lay the four in the left side."

The purple ball was resting on the lip of the left corner pocket. The cue ball was against the rail slightly below the left side pocket.

"Come on," said Arkie. "Who you think you're trying to hustle? Me, I seen you do it a hundred times."

Click.

What about hustling pool? No, man; not Arkie's style, he wasn't built for it. Patience, that's what he lacked. His nerves wouldn't take it. . . . As he stepped out the door he almost bumped smack into Clemmie. When she saw him she pranced away and made as if to hurry on.

"Hey kid, there you are," Arkie said. Made it sound jaunty. He always had to jolly her because she was five years older than he and it gave her a lot of edge. She continually put him off his stride, so that he felt like a little kid around her sometimes. "I been wondering where you at."

"Well, if you don't know where to find me by now you got to be pretty dumb." She had a pleasant throaty voice; it sounded like rich cloth tearing.

He hesitated. "Well, you know. I wouldn't want to come right busting in on you in your pad and screw things up."

She shrugged.

Oh goddam.

"That's all. I just don't want to ball things up."

Now at last he'd found Clemmie and he felt acutely miserable. Despite the cool early season she wore only a black skirt and a transparent nylon blouse. Through the filmy cloth he saw goose bumps on her upper arm. A breeze with a chill in it moved her odd-looking hair. "Come on," he said. "I'll buy you a cup of coffee."

She shrugged again, but came along anyway. Slowly though, so that Arkie felt he was just dragging along. She was a good four inches taller than he (that was, he thought, a lot of the problem right there) and she was wearing rickety spike heels. Each time she took a step her right ankle quivered; Arkie saw this but didn't know whether she noticed it.

They went into Dillard's Place and he ordered one black and sweet for himself and one light without for Clemmie. They sat in a slick plastic-seated booth. Dirty cotton batting bulged out of the tears.

"If you're wanting that single from last night I ain't got it with me."

O Lord, if that was how she was going to begin . . .

"How? Didn't the john pay up?"

He knew immediately he'd said the wrong thing. Because of his helpless anger.

She stared at him disdainfully; sniffed. "Jimmy, you mean? My boy friend Jimmy from last night? He's a *real* fine feller and yes he did let me have a little money for right now. But then I had to go and loan it all to Agnes. Agnes said she was having a hard time trying to make ends meet. Of course she's always talking like that but I thought I ought to help her out." She lifted her chin an inch or so but kept those green eyes on Arkie's eyes. "I don't know of nobody else that's going to."

"Yeh yeh. Don't worry about that." Arkie hadn't even been thinking about his dollar. She'd already gouged him for—what? At least ten or so. He knew he was never going to see it again. "I was just wondering how you was getting along, if you was all right."

"Just fine, thank you. Why wouldn't I be all right?"

"Nothing, no reason. I just got to wondering." This was the day he couldn't say one correct word. He looked at her, the tall thin girl with the bladelike face. Her features were as definite as if they had been chopped from a block of wood and her fine dry electric hair was unmanageable, fell about her shoulders like a handful of oat straw. She had bound a soiled green ribbon around underneath and tied it at the crown of her head in a coy bow. But it looked odd, off center. Arkie decided to make his move. It wasn't the best time, but now it didn't look to get any better. He leaned suddenly toward her, sliding his elbows across the table. He jarred his coffee cup and it slopped over, darkening his jacket sleeve. "Oh goddam." He snatched a paper napkin and dabbed disgustedly at the bright blue rayon. "Goddammit."

17

She giggled.

"What's so fuckin funny?" He got another napkin and began mopping at the table.

"You. You're pretty funny. Looks like you've sort of got the jitters."

He dropped the soggy napkin into the ashtray. "Gimme a stab."

Because she was still laughing at him she could obey without loss of face. She took a package of Chesterfields out of her worn red clutch bag.

He lit one and took a couple of deliberate puffs. He wasn't going to speak until he'd regained his composure.

She tried to get him going. "Now as you was saying—" But she began giggling again.

Why was it she every time had him by the short hairs? "Well . . ." He pulled his ear lobe. Tried a tactical change. "Look. You're a good friend of Oxie's, right? I mean, you really got some stretch with that guy, ain't you?"

"I guess I know him about as good as I need to."

"Well look. I don't see Oxie so much here of late. You know? He don't come down on Gimlet the way he used to and I was just wondering if you might ast him something for me." He caught her frown and rushed on nervously. "Of course I could ast him myself if I seen him. Me and Oxie are just like that." He crossed his fingers and held them before her face until she looked at them. "Asshole buddies. But I don't get up his way so much; little off my ground up where he is. I was thinking maybe if you was to see him before I did maybe you could ast him. It wouldn't be nothing."

"I don't know as how Oxie would want to be bothered a whole lot. He's awful busy these days, down at the courthouse and one thing and another."

"Yeah, I know Oxie's a mover, all right. You don't have to tell me about that guy. But this wouldn't take no time and it wouldn't cost him a penny, not a red cent. All I want is, if you could just ast him to let me know a little good action. I want to find me a little action that don't cost too much to set up. I don't mean just cheap, though. I can get up about a hundred without no sweat." He rode over this stark lie easily and gracefully because he didn't expect her to believe it. Not that he was trying to jive her. But this kind of lie was acceptable currency. They both knew what he meant by it. "Now that wouldn't be nothing to him. You know as good as I do how smart Oxie is. Got a hundred pieces of action buzzing around in his mind that he ain't even interested in. Just going to waste. All I need is something to give me a little start."

She kept shaking her head. "I don't think I better. I don't reckon I ought to bother Oxie with something like that. He's awful touchous these days, you don't never know. It don't take hardly nothing to set him off. . . ."

But Arkie had stopped listening; he was merely watching her mouth wiggle. He'd already known how she would answer.

". . . I declare that man is jumpy as a sack of snakes, you can't tell from one minute to the next. . . ."

Now, without preamble, Arkie made his move.

"Listen, Clemmie, if something was to happen between you and Oxie, how about letting me be your stringer?"

She was staggered, seemed tipsy for a moment. Her fierce green eyes looked slightly glassy. "What? What was that you said?"

He took a quick deep breath. "I said, if something was to happen, if something was to go wrong between you and Oxie, how about me coming on as your stringer." Arkie didn't know that he was speaking very loudly.

"What are you talking about? What in the goddam hell? You don't know what you're talking."

"I guess I do."

"I guess I don't. I know I don't. You." Was she spitting? No. But that was Arkie's impression. "You're just a silly little runt, that's all you are. You wouldn't be good for nobody for nothing."

"Why don't you think about it?" He was beginning to whine.

19

"That's all I'm astin, you just to think—"

"Shut your mouth."

She was leaving. She rose jerkily, pale with anger, and the two stainless steel spoons rattled on the bare table. She towered over him and her mouth was thin and twisted when she talked. "And you needn't to think you can talk to me like that. Like I was one of these damn Gimlet Street whores. You. That's just how fucking stupid you are."

She stalked away. Her figure looked set, harder and sharper than ever.

Arkie sat shaking. He was impotent with icy rage. He took out one of his loose cigarettes, but then stuffed it back into his pocket, crumpling it. Now he felt upon him the amused glance of the counterman and he turned about, staring at him savagely.

"What the hell *you* looking at?"

His amusement became heavier. "I'm looking at exactly nothing," he said.

Arkie got up; lurched. Clemmie not a whore; not one of your Gimlet whores, she said. Man, that had to be the wildest pipe he'd ever heard. She was the crawliest goddam maud on the turf. If a john had any sense he wouldn't touch her with a ten-foot cornstalk.

—What now, Arkie. What you up to now?

—Shut up, he says. Blow it out your ass, why don't you.

But as he ducked once more into the raucous sunlight he was wearing a cold secretive smile. He was still ahead of it, after all. He knew things she didn't know. Arkie had hard scrabbling, he had to keep his ear close to the ground, he had to know where it was at and he had to look ahead. Clemmie didn't look ahead, she thought she had it laid in the shade. And why? Because she was counting on old hotstuff Oxie to take care of her. But Arkie could see it coming, clear as a neon sign. Oxie was going to cut her loose and it wouldn't be long from now. That guy was leaving this part of the world, going up. He was going to cut loose from both Clemmie and Agnes. Agnes: she was nothing anyhow but a goddam mooch. Arkie would bet you she didn't turn up a clean fifty bucks a week. And look at Clemmie's drawbacks. All poison; tough and mean. Had a temper like a buzz saw. And how she got her kicks was stirring up and circulating little jealous intrigues among the pigs. She could start a fight standing alone in a ten-acre field. Trouble on wheels with rhinestone spokes. Arkie could see where things were going and how it was going to happen and he had to get dibs. Once the word was out that Clemmie was loose there would be gougers aplenty after her, and after Agnes too; heavies, the kind of guys Arkie couldn't go up against. Couldn't hold his own in that kind of rub; he had to get in first, that much was clear. . . . Goddammit, why couldn't she see that this was her best move? He was doing her one fat favor if she only knew it. Look. He wasn't going to smack her around or stomp her ass to get his rocks off. Arkie wasn't that kind of guy. And look. He was close in to things, knew where to find the best set-ups. Oxie was a million miles away. When she ran out and hit those days on the thin crust, who was going to stake her? How about for that matter the ten bucks he'd already staked her to? . . . Well, he'd made up his mind: he'd put it to her again. Soon. He tried to think how much time he had left, and it didn't seem much. . . . He felt a bit feverish. The sunlight was a precarious weight on his head, oppressive as thirst.

In Maxie's he ate a cheeseburger and drank a cold drink and then decided to get another sandwich. Uusually one satisfied him, but he'd had a rough morning. And so his meal used up almost all the money he'd made today. There was a game of liar's poker in progress in one of the booths and he joined it gratefully: not only a chance to pick up some dump; he could get his mind off Clemmie for a while. There were six guys at the table but Arkie had seen only one of them before. Didn't know his name or have any kind of book on him; just knew him as a hefty lug always

21

nervously snickering. So Arkie went gingerly for a time, cagey among strangers. After having made certain early on that he was a buck to the good, he idled, picking up a couple and dropping them as the mood struck him. In a while everyone had become familiar with the serial numbers of the bills they'd been playing with and they traded with Donald at the bar for a new batch. When Arkie was dealt his new bill he palmed it and substituted his lucky dollar. This bill he always carried with him and wouldn't think of spending; he didn't even count it in as part of his stake. The bids went round a couple of times with Arkie innocuously silent, and then the big giggly guy bid three sixes.

"I got to raise that. Six sixes."

"Who many?"

"Uh. Six."

"Get serious."

"Mess with a wife, You get trouble and strife," Arkie said.

They had to wonder what the hell that meant.

"Well, I'll challenge six any day of the week."

"Fair enough," said Arkie. "You want to raise it? Challenge for five dollars this here one time?"

The hefty fellow shied off for a moment. It was possible to have six identical digits in the serial number of a dollar bill, but who'd ever seen them? He considered the possibility of a ringer, but how? The barkeep had brought the bills to them.

"Five dollars, hell. What do you think I am?"

"I don't have no idea," Arkie said. "I been kind of wondering."

The big guy giggled; reddened; gave him a bad look. "Buddy, you finding out. I'll go you for five. You remember it was *six* sixes you said."

Archly: "Was it six? Um. Any you other gentlemens feel like putting up for five?"

No no. But they would challenge for the regular single. . . . Okay. . . . Everybody in?

He tossed the bill on the table. "Read em and weep."

22

The man across from him picked it up. "They're all there," he said, "every last one of them." He passed the bill to the hefty guy. "I be goddam," he said. He flung it down. "That cleans me." Gave Arkie another bad look. "It's a good thing I get paid tonight."

Arkie seemed to pay no attention when his winnings were passed to him. He picked up his talisman dollar and gazed at it as if actually seeing it for the first time. "Six damn sixes," he said. "I wouldn't never of believed it." He wagged his head. "It's for goddam sure this one's got to go out of the game." He reached into his pocket and pulled out the dollar the bartender had brought. "Here," he said, "let's trade it with a new one." And he put his lucky bill back into his pocket.

They played another half hour before breaking up. Arkie kept it exactly even, not winning and not losing. When the fellow sitting next to him rose to go he offered to buy him a final beer.

"No thank you. I got to be getting along. Later than I thought."

"Well, maybe next time," Arkie said. Feeling expansive. The guy seemed like, you know, like a pretty good john and you could never tell when you might be running into him again. A little Mazola made it that much easier.

He was feeling much happier now. His early impulse to stake himself to seven dollars had proved right; this was his lucky Friday. Even the hassle with Clemmie hadn't wrecked it completely.

But as he was going out he was stopped by Donald the barkeep.

"Okay, Arkie, I got to have me a piece of that."

"Piece of what?"

"Piece of the change you picked up. I've seen you pull that lucky six dodge in here before."

"What's it to you?"

"It's goddam enough to me. You sit in here every day taking up ass-room and conning my customers and slopping up the

23

tables. It's worth a piece of change to you just so as I don't blow the whistle on you ever time you come through the door."

The careful whine. "Aw come on, man. It ain't no harm to you."

Donald leaned toward him. "How'd you like to be kicked out of here for good and all?"

"I'll give you a single," Arkie said. "Honest to God, I didn't pull down all that much."

"Lay it right here in my hand."

Arkie forked it over, muttering savagely, but it really hadn't much daunted his spirits. You had to expect it now and then; the kickback was a routine part of the action.

Still traveling Rance Avenue. Making the rounds, making the rounds. A huge fat woman with a mottled face was standing on the sidewalk, just beneath the edge of the awning of a used-furniture store. She blocked his path. Looking up into her eyes, he felt a momentary bewilderment.

"Hello, Arkie," she said. "How about splitting a pipe with me? You want to split a pipe?"

"Not today, I gotta make hay."

He sidled around her and went on, but she'd clawed at his nerves. . . . Goddam hophead. Ooh, think of them eyes. Everything about her looked wrong. . . . Who was she anyhow? That was the worst of it; he couldn't put a name to her. Seemed like he'd seen her around the street but he couldn't place her. She knew him all right, though; stepped right up and called him by name. He felt a quick glow of pride. Damn right she knew him: everybody knows Arkie. He's a mover, people could tell he was going places, they kept their eyes on him. . . . Uhhh. Maybe that wasn't so awful good, to have everybody know your name. It meant the fuzz would know you too. They would come around balling things up simply because they could finger you.

Good news, bad news. Came down on you like rain.

He visited the Okay and the Blue Star, the Champagne Club, Tommy's Joint, Ed's, the Happy Time, Dr. Feelgood and the

24

Neptune Room. Making the rounds. He began to feel better as the sun got lower. The neon went on and the soft lights and weariness settled like veils of cobweb over the faces of the bartenders. The pigs came out in droves, batting their mascaraed eyes at any ambulatory entity not wearing a brassiere. He juiced a couple of gunghoes for three quarters, picked up a dime matching and another quarter at nineball, dropped a dime on the traveling Coke bottle. (You'd think for Godsake St. Louis would have taken it, but the john had a Tallahassee. He should have seen that.) He got a guy on the doorknob trick for half a rock. Just making the rounds. Arkie did his little dance.

He wandered back into the Ace, making the first full circle of the day. Clemmie and Teacher were sitting at a table. She was talking earnestly to him in that low rich voice and he seemed to be paying earnest attention but he was dog drunk. Arkie knew it. Why for Godsake did she want to talk to that silly bastard? Fat waste of time . . . He felt a twinge of fear. What if she told Teacher what Arkie had said? The dumb sonofabitch would mouth it all up and down the street. That would be pretty funny, oh yes it would: that Arkie himself had given out the word that Clemmie was unattached, that Oxie was going to cut her loose. Arkie would hang himself. Don't trust nobody, especially the mauds: how many times did a man have to be reminded?

"Greetings and hallucinations, brother," Teach said to Arkie.

"Howdy, gang," Arkie said.

"I ain't talking to you," Clemmie said.

"That just busts my heart," Arkie said. "I can't tell you how bad."

They resumed their jabbering. Clemmie lowered her voice so that Arkie couldn't hear.

He shrugged.

A couple of drunk johns were standing at the bowling machine. Arkie eyed them for a while, patiently gauging how far gone they were, and then he picked them up and juiced them for an easy buck and a half before they quit on him. But then he couldn't help rubbing it in. He stood with his back to the machine and jauntily tossed the plastic ball over his shoulder. The machine registered a strike. When he looked at their faces, he regretted immediately what he had done. They weren't so drunk they wouldn't remember that. He'd just had his last slice of action with those two. (It was that goddam Clemmie; she was eating his nerves up.) Trying to take the edge off the johns' resentment, he did his little dance; his loafers scraped and crackled on the gritty linoleum tile.

He sang, "Fried cornbread and cold coleslaw, I'm traveling down to Arkansas."

Arkansas: that was how Arkie got his nickname.

Arkansas . . .

Man, was there really such a place as that?

Ough.

Clemmie had found herself another fight. Some tough-looking maud in a blue dress had come over to the table and the two of them were shrieking at each other. Fur was going to fly, clawful after clawful. Teacher, the chicken bastard, wanted of course no part of it and he was trying to get away. Arkie laughed. It was worth money, watching him trying to sneak around the girls.

Suddenly the maud in the blue dress reached out and snatched at Clemmie's blouse. A button popped loose. Trying to scratch her tits off.

Not much there to scratch, Arkie reflected.

Clemmie stood up, totally enraged and searching blindly on the table for a beer bottle. But Arkie got there and lifted it out of reach.

"Wait a minute, womens," he said. "Throw some water on this here brush fire."

"Get out of my goddam way," Clemmie said.

"Simmer down. Because if you don't the cops'll come in and simmer you down. That what you want? You want the fuzz in here?"

"I'm going to bust her head in, that's all."

"Now you hush, just simmer down one damn minute. . . . What's

26

it all about anyhow? There ain't nothing worth fighting about."
He turned to the other maud. "How did this ruckus get started?"

"I'm just letting this here fleabit whore know she's going to
keep away from Jimmy. He's way too good for something like
her. Jimmy's my steady. We been steady a long time before he
ever laid eyes on her."

"I don't take that off of nobody," Clemmie said. "I'll bust her
fucking head in."

"Come on," Arkie said. "You don't want to do that. You'd
just feel bad about it later on."

He turned to the other. "Clemmie didn't know nothing about
all that. How was she going to know that? Anyhow, it don't do
no good to fight about it. Be better off if you just let it ride."

To Clemmie: "Come on. Let's go get us a cup of coffee down
at the Bluebird."

"I ain't backing down from this bitch." She flailed at the girl
halfheartedly, but the table was between them.

"Quit that," he said. "You ain't backing down, you just showing some sense for a change. Come on now." He tugged at her
arm and reluctantly she came with him. He was surprised.

At the cash register she turned. "You needn't to think you're
getting away with anything. You can make by God sure that
you're going to get yours."

"All right," said the other coolly. "I'll let you know where you
can find me." Color of victory in her voice.

Arkie led her out. At last the sun had set and the stars had
arrived. A mild breeze stirred about them as they stood uncer-
tainly on the pavement.

"I'm going back in there," Clemmie said. "I ain't letting her
get away with that."

"Calm down. She ain't worth wasting your time on. Get your
hands dirty."

They walked for a while, breathing heavily.

"Don't you worry none, buddy," Clemmie said. "I'm going to
settle with her and no two ways."

"Damn right."

27

"Look here. One of my buttons is off. I don't know where I can find one to match. . . . I'll settle with her. She'll wish she never heard of that Jimmy's name."

"Damn right. Later on, though. Make her worry about it a while first."

They sat hunched over coffee cups. The monotone glare of fluorescent lights enlarged their features. Man and woman; not many times Arkie had it like that. The Bluebird was drab and quiet and Greek, mostly an all-night coffee stop for cab drivers. You wouldn't come here for a good time: too much light and a dull juke.

He kept talking, soft and low. His mind raced. "And see, that's exactly why you need somebody like me for your steady stringer. Oxie now: he's getting too busy with other stuff to look after you right. He don't know what's going on down this way any more. Truth of it is, he's plumb got away from Gimlet. Take tonight now: if I hadn't been there to tell that bitch off, you'd of wound up in a fight." He was proud of himself, putting it like that. Once he got started he could speak as elegantly as any mayor. "You'd be up to your ass in trouble, and over something it wasn't worth dirtying your hands. A pig like that . . . Just one more good reason you need somebody like me around, somebody I mean that'll stick close. You see what I'm getting at."

She gazed into his eyes and smiled sweetly. "What if I was to tell Oxie what you said, how you were talking to me?"

He leaned away from her, contorting his body angrily against the back of the booth.

"Goddammit, Clemmie . . ."

Sometimes it seemed that all she was good for was to ball up the pitch. She had that grainy streak in her. . . . His mind ran furiously. Suppose she did tell, what then? It would mean one of two things: either Oxie would send some big goddam razor around to stomp Arkie, or he would simply hurry things along, seeing that the news was already out, and cut Clemmie loose that much sooner. Actually, either way was all right. If someone was coming to get him Arkie would find out long before it happened (because you can't send muscle without making noise); he would quietly duck the scene, hole up somewhere. Or if he decided to get rid of Clemmie sooner, then it would be that much sooner she'd see how Arkie was smart, really on top of things. Okay, then.

He made himself relax; yawned ostentatiously. "Go ahead and tell him. It don't make no never-mind to me."

"Ain't you afraid what he might do?" She looked at him with a newly serious curiosity.

"Oxie don't scare me none. What I been trying to tell you, he don't know this territory near as good as I do. Got too many other things on his mind. He don't scare me even a little bit."

She kept watching him. Maybe after all she was beginning to get the message. "Anyway," she said, "sooner or later you'd have to settle up with him. There wouldn't be no way out of that."

Sometimes it occurred to Arkie that maybe Clemmie wasn't hampered by a lot of brain power.

"No, now dammit, don't get it all fouled up. I ain't trying to ball up any arrangements you-all might have. All I'm saying is, if it does happen, you know who you can come to. It ain't no more than just a friendly offer."

She seemed mollified. "Well. I'll remember what you said."

"Good. Fine and dandy. That's all in the world I want you to do, keep it in mind."

"Let's get out of here." She looked about distastefully. "This place is so dead it's spooky."

"All right," he said. "But let's don't go back to the Ace. I'm getting good and sick of that joint." Always the diplomat; he knew if she spotted the pig in the blue dress she'd start the fight where it left off.

"Let's go down to the Bunny. Maybe Agnes might be there. I need to see Agnes about something."

"Let's go."

The Big Bunny had come alive, crowded and noisy and wet. When they entered they were greeted loudly, beerily welcome.

The regular crowd had gathered and they saluted all familiar faces more or less in the same fashion.

Clemmie went immediately to sit on someone's lap.

Someone yelled at him, "Hey Arkie, tell us a lie."

"Wash your mouth out," he yelled back. "I never told a lie in my life."

"Arkie. Match you for the juke."

"Match you for the quarter," he countered.

He ran up a score of 5837 on the Space Patrol pinball machine and put seventy-five cents into his pocket.

You couldn't keep him down now, he couldn't remember when he'd been so happy. He felt confident about his whole life and he offered to match Squelch for that five spot, but now the stolid barkeep chickened out of the bet and Arkie ribbed him unmercifully. "And I thought you was a sporting man," he said. Even when Clemmie gouged him for another single and left with a drunk john he didn't much mind.

"Screw the women, screw the law, I'm traveling down to Arkansas." He did his little dance.

In a while he felt hot and too keyed up and he stepped out on the sidewalk to settle his nerves before taking another round at the pinball machine. He saw that the sky was filled with cool stars. Suddenly it occurred to him that this street, Gimlet Street, could take you anywhere in the world, it was joined to all the other streets there were. He shook his head, grinning. Arkie couldn't go. This was his territory. He was chained to Gimlet and he was chained to Clemmie, that green-eyed girl he was so helplessly in love with.

"River gonna rise, creek gonna thaw, I'm traveling down to Arkansas."

30

Clemmie

Consider Clemmie.

(Poor speck of flotsam.)

She's thin as a knife blade, an efficient-looking girl. But it's not a healthy efficiency, all got by nervous energy. The rate she's going makes you want to bet that the machine will break down before she's twenty-one. Now she's nineteen, and three years already she's been on the turf, balling the johns on Gimlet.

At noon on this uncertain Saturday she lies thinking how many friends she has, good friends who are truly concerned for her welfare; but two hours later she's angry and defiant, reflecting that she hasn't a friend in the world, not a single person gives a damn. The barometer of her temperament is always violent, goes up and down like an elevator.

She was going to get out of bed at eleven, actually swung her long bony feet over, but the cold slick thrill of the linoleum tile dismayed her and she flopped back and pulled up the sheet. She struggled for comfort, unbunching her dingy pink slip beneath her and plumping the pillow again. For half an hour she lay staring at the splotched ceiling and thinking easy silly thoughts, daydreaming of men and clothes and powerful cars. The sunlight through the green cotton print curtains grew bright, then dim, then bright once more. Now and then she hummed scraps of juke songs and occasionally she giggled. Inspected her fingernails. At last she rose and went to the bathroom.

Returning to the bedroom she stood looking almost in bewilderment about her. She smoothed the slip along her skinny flanks. Her pussy itched and she scratched.

What was that a sign of?

Coughed, and laid her hand on her throat. It occurred to her that she couldn't remember Horace's departure very clearly and she hurried to the bedside table and jerked open the drawer. You had to make sure, always. She saw with relief that the money was still there. Seventeen dollars and something, counting her own change and the dollar she had got from Arkie . . . So after all, that Horace wasn't so bad, not nearly as bad as he liked to make out. She wondered perversely if that was his true name. She bet it was because he had paused a moment after he'd told it, as if he'd planned to say something else but at the last minute it had slipped his mind.

Why were they so tender about their names? She didn't care, nobody gave a good goddam what a john's real name was.

Sighed, and went to the dressing table to begin the repair job . . . She was proud that it didn't take her all that long. Agnes now was different; took her simply hours to put herself back together after even an easy night. She watched herself in the mirror and considered that she actually looked pretty good: had a model's figure, a model's face. Several times she'd been thinking she might go into that, it couldn't be so hard to learn. She was young, after all, and she had her whole future before her.

She was a live one.

But, God, that hair.

She fought with it resentfully, almost tearing it with the comb. If it wasn't so fine she'd get it cut short like Audrey Hepburn in that television movie. But it was fine and dry; if it was short she'd look like a partly bald porcupine. Horace had been ragging her about her hair (the son of a bitch) but when she told him he was as fat as a toad frog he got mad. Kind of guy that could dish

32

it out but couldn't take it. For a moment she'd thought he might hit her. You had to go careful. Usually the guy had a load on, and you couldn't tell what he'd do. And there was a whole army of them would hit you just for kicks.

What the hell anyway. She could take care of herself, she was armed. Oxie had loaned her a pistol, a little 25-caliber Eye-talian gun. And she even had a bullet for it. —Oh Jesus, what did she know about guns? If she ever tried to fire it, she'd probably shoot her toes off. Oxie had said that all she would ever have to do if she needed to protect herself was just show it. Show him a gun, and the biggest meanest john in the world would back down. Especially if it was a woman, Oxie said; it was the fact that it was a woman with a gun that really scared them.

He was smart, Oxie. Arkie had said that he was moving along, climbing out of Gimlet Street. She wondered if it was true. (Arkie was pretty smart too, in his own runty way.) What did you climb *to,* though, if you left Gimlet? The fine hotels, she supposed, and the rich clubs. Wine in long-stemmed glasses and big pink convertibles and gambling men in tuxedos. What was so great about all that? In the bed it's just as sweet anywhere, even at the North Pole probably.

She thought. Now and then she'd wondered about how the Eskimos did it.Teach had told her that they rubbed noses, and he'd been fairly sober for a change. Well okay. But it didn't seem to get you anywhere very fast, rubbing noses.

Five presentable outfits she had, but two of them were at the cleaner's now. One of her thousand resentments: she could easily carry them to the cleaner's herself, but it was part of the whole residence deal that the Braceboro Arms would handle cleaning and of course they gouged her unmercifully. She bet she paid twice as much. And the work was getting sloppier and sloppier. . . .

She took from the tall ungainly wardrobe a light blue—"ice blue," the salesman had called it—dress, the one least soiled. It wasn't what you'd call sexy, no, but yesterday had been cooler than she'd expected and she'd felt chilly all day. She put it on and went again to the omnipresent mirror and looked. Well, not *too* bad. Maybe like a snotty secretary. Like a department store supervisor, maybe. For a while after she'd bought this dress she thought that perhaps she'd made a mistake but now it was almost her favorite. It looked businesslike and, man, Clemmie meant business.

Hoo.

She was a live one.

How does it do? Everything all set?

She pulled the ice blue flat over her ass, leaned close to peer at the mouth. Speck there under her eye?

Ough, that hair.

Where *did* you get that set? Discount sale in the hayfield?

She got the money out of the night table drawer and put ten of it in a hat box from the top shelf of the wardrobe. Inside the hat box it looked very happy: seven tens and a twenty. If ninety dollars didn't make Oxie cheerful, he'd better go out and hire Santy Claus, it was the only way he'd do any better.

—But what about for Clemmie? These are perilous days, no one will deny it. Surely a hard-working girl has got to put by a little to fall back on.

—Oh, here and there she's squirreled a bit.

Teacher was holding nearly one hundred dollars for her. She felt that she could trust Teach; once you got to know him you found a surprising streak of the gentleman. Teach was full of surprises, actually. . . . She knew in her heart though that there was a sad story there, probably a long time ago some no-account girl had cruelly busted his heart and that was what drove him to drink so hard. She nodded wisely. She was going to get him to tell her all about it sometime; it would be real sad but real interesting. . . .

Checked her purse. Round brass compact, lipstick, three shredded wads of Kleenex, loose pennies, the billfold empty except for the I.D. card she'd made out (it came with the billfold) and two snapshots of soldiers (now she wasn't certain she was putting the right names with the right photos), plastic cylinder of stale Vicks inhalant, half a package of Dentyne, pack of Chesterfields. So: she stuffed in the seven dollars and the change.

Hoo hoo. How about one big bright final smile for the mirror?

Ready to meet the world on its own terms. On any terms.

In the mornings she felt uncertain of her balance on her spike heels but she took the stairs nevertheless. The elevator frightened her, narrow and dim as a coffin, and in its descent it shook and rattled like an oak in a windstorm. No pleasantries in the lobby, the desk clerk and the bellhops noted her with listless gaze and she ignored them altogether. —Christ Jesus, why couldn't they at least dust these damn potted plants?

Outside the weather felt warmer and though she was immediately grateful she was vexed because she could have worn her skirt and blouse combination comfortably today. No she couldn't; there was a button missing. (That goddam bitch, she was still by God going to get hers.) She felt hungry and sociable; wanted somebody to talk to while she ate breakfast. Agnes wouldn't be around for a good while yet; it took her hours to get started. (But you had to consider how much labor it cost to get her in lookable shape.) She thought of Teacher. He would be at the Ace; that was his starting point and often enough he never got any farther. She turned the corner.

John was busy behind the bar, readying the joint for the lunch crowd, but she knew he'd stop for her. She was a steady breakfast customer. She fluttered onto a bar stool next to Teacher and ordered bacon and eggs and toast and coffee. "Don't scramble them eggs too hard."

"Okay, Clemmie. I ought to know by now." He finished stacking plates before he went to get her order.

"Is that one a good one?" she asked.

Teacher flipped up the cover of the paperback. *Galactic Patrol* by E. E. Smith, Ph.D. Bright red and yellow printing, weird-looking creature brandishing a battle-axe, rocket ships plowing through a sky like tomato sauce. "I guess it's all right," he said. "Better than I thought it was going to be."

35

"I don't believe in that future stuff." The idea came upon her suddenly, but having thought of it she believed it wholeheartedly.

"That ain't the point," he said. "It's not what's *going* to happen, it's what *might* happen. That's the difference."

"Anything can happen," she said, "but I don't believe in it."

"Maybe you're right. Anyhow, it's nothing special." He slid the book into the pocket of the soiled corduroy jacket he always wore. "Did you have a good night?"

She gave him a hard steady look but his expression was pleasant; he didn't mean anything special. "Just one more Friday night. How come you're asking?"

"No real reason. I was thinking maybe that crazy-ass broad had caught up with you and tried to give you a hard time."

She remembered now: Teach had been there, sitting at the table with her. At least he was there when it started; she couldn't remember where he was when it had got hot. Then it was all Arkie. "Huh." Nodded her head slowly. "I reckon she damn well knew better. I never did see her again. I reckon she knew better than to come messing with me."

"She kept on strutting around here for a while. She was blowing off pretty impressive."

"Goddam fatass bitch. She runs into me, she won't talk so big. We still got something to settle, me and her."

"I never said a word to her. I just let her run on, and I kind of kept laughing to myself. Said to myself, Woman, you ought to count yourself lucky Clemmie ain't here to hear that kind of talk. She wouldn't let much of that trash go on."

"Don't you worry none about it, buddy. I'll settle with her."

"That's what I figured. I figured she'd be talking a different kind of way before she seen the end of it. . . ." He drank from his beer can and watched her spoon eggs into her mouth. "Oxie come by looking for you."

"Oxie?" It hit her so suddenly that she blushed. A rubbery bit of egg dropped in her lap. "When?"

"Little while."

36

"Where did he say he was going?"

Teacher shrugged. "He didn't say, but wherever it was he went he was pretty soon there. He's a hurrying kind of feller. He did say he'd be back in a little while."

"Back here? In the Ace?"

"That's what the man said."

She smiled and nodded. Why did she bother to listen to Arkie? If Oxie was looking for her, it just showed how much that runty bastard knew about anything. She and Oxie had it square between them, steady as a rock. He wouldn't turn Clemmie loose. It wasn't like true love or romance (sometimes she wondered unimaginable thoughts about Oxie), but there was a real thing there. It was an . . . an *understanding*. Understanding was a fine word. She nodded again.

"What did he say he wanted?"

Teacher chuckled. "Well, I don't know why it is, Clemmie, but Oxie don't bother to tell his business to just everybody he runs into."

She grinned. Now she was happy. She pushed her scoured greasy plate to the edge of the counter. John brought her another cup of coffee and she fished out a cigarette and smoked with an expansive display of pleasure. Ah, she was secure, cared for; so many friends she had and all of them so different. Teacher, Oxie, Horace, Jimmy, Squelch, and even that dopey squirt Arkie, if she felt like counting him in. She thought about how it was she alone who in some mysterious way bound all of them together. She felt relaxed, and spoke to Teacher in a speculative tone of voice: "I wish I read books like you do. I guess you must learn a whole lot, reading all the time like that. That's what I always wanted to do, get me a big load of books and take some time off and just read and read and read. But Lord, I don't know when. Seems like I'm always doing something."

"Oh, I don't know," Teacher said slowly. "It don't seem to me like I'm learning so much. Most of these books is plain trash. Something to pass the time with is all . . ."

37

She had stopped listening because Oxie had entered. He paused for a moment in the doorway, obviously intent to impress his emblematic magnificence upon whoever might be inside. He was wearing dark brown gabardine slacks and highly polished dark shoes with buckles at the sides and a heavy-looking moleskin jacket. A dark green suede tie hung down a soft white shirt with a rolled collar; the tie was clasped with a gold horseshoe tack. On his right hand a broad gold ring with a large diamond in a triangular setting. He used the bearing of a man who is always conscious of the effect of his presence in a room, and he came forward with a light easy tread, almost a mincing step. Had about him the confidence of a boxer who knows he will polish off his opponent this round or the next.

"Why howdy there, stranger," Clemmie cried gaily. "I ain't seen you it seems like years. Where in the world you ever been to—Arkansas?"

"Clemmie," he said. Just the one word—how like him that was!—in his low, slightly thick voice that for some weird reason always reminded Clemmie of the dense risen cream being poured from the top of the milk bottle.

He motioned toward a table in a corner and went to it. She followed, bobbing happily in his wake. He pulled out a chair for her and she sat as gracefully as she could manage. See that? That was the difference between Oxie and everyone else she knew. Class, was what you called it. . . . He showed two casual fingers for coffee before turning to her.

"What?" she said. It happened like this every time: when he began talking to her she became confused and couldn't understand a word. Trouble was, she was always concentrating on the relaxed olive face with that moustache as black as jeweler's velvet and the dark brown eyes with the cat-yellow lights in them.

"I just asked how everything was going, Clemmie. Are you keeping yourself alive?"

Hoo. Clemmie gets more than just by. Clemmie's a live one.

"I been doing fine, she said. "Of course now, I missed *you*. Seems like it's been an awful long time."

He sighed gently. "Always the same old thing, sweetheart. Business and more business. Just never get the chance no more to sit down and chat with my old friends. A real shame."

Old friends: that was the kind of talk she liked to hear. She felt that she'd been stroked like a kitten. If Arkie could hear Oxie now, the little runt wouldn't be making such a damn fool of himself. "Well," she said, "I hear tell your business is going real good. Everybody keeps talking about how good you're doing. You're a real lucky person."

He shook his head slowly, reproachfully. "Clemmie, don't you ever make that kind of mistake, you're too intelligent to believe in that. It's not luck that brings success, it's hard work. I've been working very hard, you know."

"Oh yes," she said hastily, "I know that." But in her heart she knew it was luck. For her it had to be luck because that added another splendor to Oxie. Any dumb john could work hard. Luck was part of Oxie's class.

"And you've got to be willing to take on responsibilities. That's one of the things that makes it so tough. You can't sit around and let other people make your decisions."

"I can see that." She nodded, but she wasn't certain that she was supposed to reply. His words had got quieter and quieter, as if he were really talking to himself.

He caught himself up. Briskly to business. "Well now. You say things have been going pretty good. No complaints?"

"I guess not. Everything's been fine."

And then she commenced her recital of obscure grievances: she had been mistreated by the bartenders in the Big Bunny, in Maxie's, the Champagne Club, the Happy Time, the Starlite. She had been sick on her stomach a couple of days and couldn't get out to see nobody, and them blue pills she'd took had just made her feel all the worse. Nearly sprained her ankle, Wednesday week it was, when one of her heels had busted off just like that. (Snapped her fingers. Peppy.) And Agnes was always borrowing money from her and you never knew if and when she'd get it back. And then there had been a number of fights: someone else always started them for the most mysterious and unjust reasons. The truth of it, these Gimlet Street whores were laying for her. Luckily Clemmie had come off victorious in every one of them, but it was a trial, to have to keep defending herself. And then Arkie that little runt midget had been driving her straight up the wall with all of his crazy jabber. You should have heard the crazy things he'd been saying about her and Oxie.

"Wait a minute," Oxie said. "Who is this Arkie person?"

Oh, he was just some little sawed-off squirt that was always around juicing the johns with his little penny ante games. Nobody paid him no never-mind. He didn't count for anything.

"Wait a minute," Oxie said. "Blond-haired kid? Wears a shiny blue jacket with white stripes on the sleeves?"

She was startled. "That's him, that's Arkie. Why? Is he a buddy of yours?"

He laughed softly. "Well, not hardly. But I've seen him around. Somehow I got him pegged as a guy that might probably be needing me one of these first days but that I probably wouldn't be able to do him any good."

"Ha ha."

Oxie meant that one of these days he expected to see Arkie down in the jailhouse; he'd be wanting a bondsman but Oxie wouldn't be able to go his bail. He'd already spotted Arkie as a guy who'd never have any money.

"What kind of things has this character been saying?"

She took a deep breath, toyed with her coffee spoon. This was her best chance to find out exactly where she stood with Oxie, but she was nervous about asking. Finally she told him what Arkie had figured out and about his proposition to take her over. Then she waited tensely for his reaction.

He was silent momentarily, then began laughing gently. "That kid's got some wild imagination. He ought to go on the television."

"He's just a dumb runt." She was giggling with pure relief. "There don't nobody pay him any mind."

Now he became serious, almost grave. "Well, I just wanted to find out how you were getting along, Clemmie. To see if you were doing all right. I've got a little business that'll keep me busy the next hour or so, but I thought maybe we could arrange to meet after a while and get our own little business out of the way."

"Sure, that will be fine," she said. "I got to tell you though, I don't have too much money. Like I was saying, I been laid up sick here off and on and I ain't got as much as I might have."

"Don't worry your pretty head about it," Oxie said. "I know how things go sometimes. But I want you to know I've got a world of confidence in you. You just do the best you can, and I'll meet you at two o'clock. I've been wanting to take you out to lunch and around, you know; sometime you and me could just make a day of it. We'll get together and do it up brown one of these first days. Right now though I've got this little business to tend to. Seems like there's always something in the way."

"Oh, that's all right. It's awful sweet of you to think of it. But anyhow I just finished eating, so I wouldn't be able to."

"See you at two then." He rose and held her chair as she too got up.

"Back here?"

"No, let's get together down at the Big Bunny. That would be closer for me. I want to see Agnes too if I can."

Teacher had opened up his book again and was reading. On his way out Oxie stopped, turned over the cover and had a look. "How come you want to read this kind of trash? Doesn't do you any good. Complete waste, I'd be thinking."

"It's just something to pass the time," Teach said. "I don't take it serious."

"Well, I'll tell you a book," Oxie said. "A book you can really get a lot of good out of. It's called *How to Win Friends and Influence People*. I've read it I guess at least two times."

And he left.

"Thanks for the tip, Oxie," Teacher said. Talking to the closed door.

Clemmie sat down to talk with Teach a few minutes before going on her way. "You know, I bet that's real good advice he give you about that book. You can trust Oxie," she began.

Had she ever been so happy as she was now? She certainly couldn't remember when. She felt bubbly and she walked along with a haughty step, too filled with good resolutions to take notice of the people on the sidewalk. She thought that she ought to look up Agnes and tell her that Oxie was expecting to meet her. (And for God's sake help the girl find a little more presentable appearance.) She stopped in the Starlite. The lunch crowd was thinning out now and Agnes was nowhere to be seen. But Arkie was present. (Arkie was omnipresent.) He rolled a small pair of red plastic dice on the counter, then scooped up a quarter and dropped it into his pocket. He slapped his john—who looked sort of feeble-minded—lightly on the shoulder and told him, Well old-timer, you can't win them all. Clemmie knew how he jollied them at the end so he could juice them again next week.

He caught sight of her. "Hey there ugly girl. What's new in the world?"

"I ain't talking to you," she said.

"Oh goddam," Arkie said. "Again?"

She left him standing there.

For Agnes she searched no longer. She decided instead to celebrate, she was going to buy something for herself. Who, after all, deserved it more? Clemmie was a live one and a hard worker too. Time she thought of herself for a change. She returned to the hotel and got down the hat box and very carefully counted the money again. Then she removed the ten she had contributed when she got up this morning. It was going to be a celebration: she would buy some jewelry or maybe some perfume or . . . something. She didn't need to imagine what it would be at the moment. Oxie wouldn't mind, she bet that even if she told him he wouldn't

42

mind. A girl in her position had to look her best; it was the only thing in the world she had to get by on.

She folded the eighty dollars into a tight packet and wedged it into her billfold and let the other ten flutter loose in her clutch bag. She left the hotel still not having decided exactly what it was she was shopping for—not that it mattered, the shopping itself was the pleasure. And with this notion in mind she walked the five blocks to Penney's department store. Always when she went on a personal errand like this she was agreeably oppressed by a feeling of excitement and clutter, of a gay confusion. She went from Penney's to Woolworth's, where she stopped for coffee, and then on to Ivey's and Belk's. The hour arrowed by; it was already 1:40. She had seen several things she'd liked (especially that little gold fleur-de-lis pin with the blue stone), but she couldn't make up her mind to buy anything. And now she began to feel apprehensive about her sudden spree. She thought of Oxie. Ninety dollars really wasn't so very much money, and eighty dollars was less. Now it seemed conspicuously less. Oxie was truly a gentleman, but you didn't want to cross him. Manners only go so far. Suppose he started talking to Teacher and Teacher happened to let it drop about the money she had saved back from her earnings. —When Teacher was drunk you'd be wise not to trust him too far.—That would not be good. It was hard to believe that Oxie would hurt her for a little bit of money or even that he'd be really angry. But it would not be good.

(Not that he couldn't hurt her if he thought he had reason enough. How vividly she remembered his talent in this direction.)

So once again she walked, past the minuscule triangular park filled with people waiting for buses; turned left at the S&W cafeteria and walked past the bank and beneath the flickering marquee of the Imperial Theater and past a line of greasy spoons; turned left once more at the bronze equestrian statue of Zebulon Johns, Patriot and Philanthropist. She came to Gimlet Street and started downhill. It had turned quite warm and she breathed heavily from the unwonted exercise and her unseasonable outfit. Earlier she had been loitering because she didn't want to arrive early for the appointment (what every woman knows, that a show of eagerness puts a man off), but now she had to hurry in order not to be too late. Besides, she needed to take a leak. All that coffee.

Oxie waited in the Big Bunny with an untouched glass of beer before him. His expression was even more grave and thoughtful than usual. Clemmie waved to him as she went past into the bathroom. Before she came out she observed herself thoroughly in the mirror. (Not so bad, huh? You can see right off that she's a live one. Ough, where did you get that hair?)

She came out and sat down with him, all out of breath. "I hope I didn't keep you waiting too long," she said. "I'm awful sorry about how I'm late."

"Don't worry about it." He was murmuring darkly, she could hardly hear. There was something odd.

"Well, I know how busy you are and everything."

"Nothing. Don't worry about it. Can I buy you a drink?"

"No thank you. I don't hardly never drink beer or alcohol, you know. Girl can't do that and still keep her figure. Blows you up like a balloon. . . . You know I wouldn't never say nothing bad about Agnes, I don't do that, but it's really awful the way she lets herself go. Now of course it's none of my business, but maybe she oughtn't to drink so hard. Maybe you could say something to her. She'll listen to you any time and she won't pay me no mind at all. None."

"I couldn't find Agnes." His voice was still very quiet. "To tell the truth, I really didn't look."

"Did you go over to her place? She's probably just laying up."

Clemmie lived at the Braceboro Arms, Agnes lived at the Lexington.

"I didn't have the time."

Something was bothering Oxie, no doubt about it. He wasn't unhappy: in fact underneath it all he seemed happily excited. But he appeared more serious than usual; his talking was grave and measured. She thought that perhaps the money would please him and she took it out, including the ten dollars she had at first

44

planned to spend on herself, and spread it on the table before him.

"Well, here it is," she said. "Like I told you before, it ain't as much as it probably might be because I been laid up sick now and again. But it's not too bad, either: ninety dollars there."

He looked at it. It seemed a long time before he spoke. Finally he gave the money back to her, nudging it across the tabletop with his fingertip. "You keep this money, Clemmie."

"What?"

"You'd better keep it."

"What for?" She was frightened.

"You might come in need of it." He folded his smooth plump hands on the table and leaned toward her. He loomed heavy in her vision. "You remember what we were talking about before? About what that little Arkie character was telling you? Well, it wasn't so then—I wasn't lying to you—but it is so now."

"What in the world are you trying to say?"

"I've decided to pull out of it," he said. "It's as simple as that."

"You're joking me, ain't you?"

"No."

"But why, for Chrisake? Pulling out just like that. Why?"

He spoke more loudly. "What does it matter why? I've decided to do it and I'm going to do it. Be a lot better for you if you just leave it like it is." He had been angered for a moment, but now he resumed his usual calm. "I'll add another ten spot to that pile," he said. "That'll give you an even hundred."

She struck with her open hand at the line of bills, scattering them on the table and floor. "Hell with the money. What about me? What you expect I'm going to do?"

"Oh, you'll make out fine, a girl with your looks."

"Shit."

"It's not all that bad."

She was close to crying, from anger, from self-pity. She began gathering the money again and she bent over to retrieve some bills from the floor. She knew that her face was red and her eyes were red and she didn't want to look directly at Oxie. "Tell me this," she said. "Who's going to talk to the cops for me? They'll hassle me every minute. Who's going to keep these goddam bar-hops in line? They'll gouge me for every penny I get my hands on. Who's going to keep them in line? Tell me that."

"It's not as bad as you're trying to make out," he said. "There's a lot of people I might worry about but Clemmie's not one of them. You're too smart and good-looking. It's a cinch bet you can take care of yourself without anybody's help."

"What I can't figure out is why. I never done you no dirt, never knocked down on you. I can't figure out why."

"It doesn't matter why. The truth is, I can't afford to handle you any more. But it doesn't matter."

"I know what you mean, you ain't got to pussyfoot. You think because you've got this jail bond con operating you've got to be too good for somebody like me. You're thinking how to stay in sweet with them high and mighty bastards down at the court-house. Think you're too good for me any more." Her voice had acquired an edge, became raw and piercing. "It makes you sick to the stomach, don't it, just to sit here with me?"

He shrugged. "I offered you that ten spot, take it or leave it. As far as I'm concerned, it's all finished."

She told him what he could do with the money. "You can't shit me," she said. "You think you can treat me like one of these goddam Gimlet Street whores. I know who you are, buddy, and I know where you come from. You ain't no better than anybody else around here. You might have lucked up into a fast con or two, but you ain't no better than me. You ain't no different."

He shrugged once more and rose, sighing. "Clemmie," he said, "that's all there is. Take care of yourself."

She sat staring at the wall until she heard the door close behind Oxie. A single burning tear appeared on her cheek as if it had condensed there. She allowed it to roll and fall onto the breast of the ice blue dress. Then she picked up the money and wadded it and stuffed it into her clutch bag. In her hands the bills felt like so much waste paper. She rose dizzily and went into the bathroom to repair her face. In the patchy mirror she watched herself for a long time. Oxie was wrong about her looks. (He was full of it anyway.) Her face was too thin and sharp, it was a lonesome-looking face. She kneaded one bony hand in the other. Now it was all clear to her: she hadn't a single friend, nobody in the whole world gave a good goddam.

When she came out of the bathroom she was hurrying as if she was late for an urgent appointment, but she had no earthly idea where she was headed. Away from where she had sat talking with Oxie, that was enough.

"Wait a minute, Clemmie," the barkeep said.

"What is it you want, Squelch?"

The fat red-haired man gazed at her with his calm blue eyes. Always he kept his bland manners, always he took his time. "What was all that ruckus going on, you and Oxie?"

"I can't see it's any of your business."

"Can't never tell," he said. "Might turn out it is my business, one of these first days."

"Well, I can tell you right now it ain't none of your business, ain't never going to be. Just keep your goddam nose out."

He smiled a slight and waning smile. "I'll be seeing you around," he said.

The bewildered rage in her had congealed to a cold voiceless fury. So they had started in on her already. Was this the way it was going to be from here on out? She'd show them that it wouldn't take much for her to set them by God straight. . . . What finally got her goat was that there was no reason for it, except Oxie getting so stuck up. And just leaving her cold like he did, and not Word One about what to expect. That little bastard Arkie had got it exactly right. She wondered how he knew. How come he was so smart? She wondered if Arkie had talked to Oxie, if this was one of Arkie's cons, some way or another. . . . No no: if Oxie was too stuck up for Clemmie you know he wouldn't give spitting time to Arkie.

And now what? It occurred to her that Agnes didn't know yet. Oxie had left it up to her to inform Agnes. Well, fuck that. His mess, let him clean it up.

47

She wandered dazedly into the Happy Time and started drinking. After four or five beers in a row, she sent a taxi driver down to buy her a pint of blended. Today was after all a holiday; it was the jubilee. Anyway, she'd been planning a little celebration, hadn't she? She drifted to the jukebox and began searching the titles for something sweet and pretty. While she was bending over the machine a guy came up and put his hands on her waist.

"Play something real nice, sweetheart," he said.

She paused a moment, collecting her anger, before she turned to face him. "Get your goddam hands off of me," she said. "Don't get it in your goddam silly head I'm one of your Gimlet Street whores. I'll blow the whistle so fast you won't know what hit you."

He stepped back; his face burned scarlet. "Excuse *me,* honey. I don't want no trouble. I mistook you for somebody I knowed."

"I know what you mistook. You just better keep clear of me." She turned and punched the jukebox buttons savagely, playing all the wrong songs. —But turning upon the john had momentarily lightened her mood. That was a real luxury.

She kept at it and by five o'clock she was fairly slotched, though still in control of herself and slyly calculating. She felt the gaze of the barkeep; he was gauging her, he was getting ready to throw her out.

He came to the table. "Clemmie, it looks to me like you've about had more than your share. I got to think about my license, you know. Why don't you go home and catch yourself a nap for a little while?"

"Don't get your bowels in an uproar. Bring me a cup of coffee and a Alka-Seltzer and fix me a plate of ham and eggs."

She almost giggled at the relief that showed on his face. She'd faked him out. Ha, she knew what she was doing, she was nobody's staggering drunk. She could keep going like this all night and it wouldn't bother her. Water off the duck's back . . . But when the food arrived she had only cold distaste for it and had to force herself to eat.

Now she had sobered a bit and had become bored and irritated and melancholy. Where was the action? It was Saturday night but in here it was still gloomy as a church. She stuffed the clumsy pint bottle into her clutch bag and set out to make the rounds.

In Maxie's, the Champagne Club, in Fred's Place and the Playboy she couldn't find a single soul worth talking to. It was as she'd always suspected: she hadn't a friend in the world.

The eastern sky had darkened to an inky purple and the west was streaked broadly with red and orange, sharp blue mountains shouldering into these streaks. Overhead a few lonesome stars had leaked through; and a breeze, warm and dampish, wandered the streets, tightening her dress against the backs of her legs. Did you ever think how probably the same breeze was blowing in New York and Texas and all over the United States of America? Suddenly Clemmie remembered that she owned two hundred dollars. What she ought to do was tell this Mickey Mouse town to go screw itself and buy herself a bus ticket. Catch the first Greyhound to California. There was nothing to hold her here, not a thing any more, except the fact that she had been born here, in a filthy apartment on Flint Street, and any other place she tried to imagine seemed as flossy and unbelievable as a Technicolor movie.

In the Starlite she spotted Arkie playing the pinball machine with a soldier. The soldier watched glumly through horn-rimmed glasses as Arkie turned the score digits over and brought them back to 205 again.

"Come on soldier man, Beat that if you can."

Clemmie spoke to the soldier. "Don't do it, honey, don't let him con you. He's the biggest con I know of. There ain't nobody can take him on one of these machines."

The soldier handed Arkie two quarters. "Lady, I couldn't argue with you," he said.

"Aw, don't pay her no mind," Arkie said. "I happened to hit a lucky streak, is all. Let's go one more time."

"No thank you."

"One more time. We'll go for one quarter this time."

"No thank you. I just as soon drown my money in the river." He stuffed his hands in his pockets and went to the bar.

"Goddam you anyhow," Arkie said. "I was just getting him ready. I could of juiced him for another four. Easy as slicing an apple."

"Ooh is my ittle boy mad at Clemmie? Is my ittle boy pissed off cause Clemmie scared away his soldier-john?—I was just joking you. Come on over and I'll buy you a cold drink."

"*You*'ll buy *me*? Man, it's got to be the end of the world."

Nevertheless, he followed her to the table, sipped slowly at his Pepsi and watched in astonishment as she ordered a set-up and took the bottle from her clutch bag and proceeded to pour herself a drink.

"By God, it *is* the end of the world. I don't think I ever seen you take a drink."

"World's a big old place." She pronounced her words with finicky precision; the alcohol was beginning to reach her again. "I bet there's a whole mess of things you ain't seen."

He grunted. Obviously he didn't believe that statement. "What's got into you anyhow? I seen you this afternoon and you wouldn't give me air in a jug, and now tonight you buy me a cold drink and come on sweet like honey. You think you can just turn me on and off like a spigot?"

Archly: "Well . . ." She giggled knowingly.

He shrugged. How the hell could he deny it? She had him on the barb end, could haul him in anytime she pleased. It was simply too bad that she knew it so well. "You awful happy, seems like."

"I ain't happy, there ain't no way I'm happy. But I figure what's the use of carrying on sad? It don't do no good, so you might as well be cheery."

"You sound like you been talking to Teacher."

"It ain't nothing to be ashamed of, talking to Teacher. He's got more sense than some people I know."

"I ain't never seen the sense in him."

"At least he knows how to read. That's more than I can say for some people."

He was steadfastly ignoring her significant look. He shrugged.

It was an impasse. How was she going to begin talking to him again? Arkie, he always made it so hard on you. There were things he could learn from Teach, if he only cared.

She made a stab at it. "Did you happen to see Oxie today?"

"I heard he was around, is all. I heard you two got in some sort of ruckus, but I never did see the man."

"Who told you that, about us having a fight?"

"I don't remember who it was. That was just the word around, that you-all were going at it."

Oh, for God's sake. Christ. It had already started, it was like watching a car roll into a brick wall. They were already on to her. No such thing as a girl's private life on Gimlet Street. She bet the whole goddam town was talking about it.

"Well, don't you worry," she said. "He'll get his. He's got a little something coming to him."

"What happened?"

"Why don't you tell me?" she said. "Seems like you know everything already."

"I heard there was a ruckus. I didn't hear what it was about."

She breathed deep and plunged in. "That damn Oxie, he's got so stuck-up . . . I'd like to know where he thinks he gets off. He ain't no better than anybody else. Happened to run into a pile of luck, that's all. I know people right here on this street that wouldn't spit on him when he first started out. No reason for him to act so big."

Arkie shook his head. "But that's the way things go. Whether it's right or wrong no use to talk about."

"I don't see that it's like that. He's always talking about working hard, about how you got to work your way up. All that stuff, it don't mean nothing. He don't work, he wouldn't strike a lick at a snake. He just had some luck."

51

"Maybe you're right."

She gave him a shrewd glance. "You ain't been talking to him, have you?"

If it was Arkie who put into Oxie's head the notion to turn loose, she wouldn't have anything more to do with the runty bastard. She'd cut his ass dead forever.

"Not me, I ain't seen him. We used to be good buddies, me and Oxie, but here of late I ain't hardly seen him at all. Like you was saying, he's got awful stuck-up."

She nodded, feeling better. About that one thing she had been right at least. For a while she'd been thinking she didn't know a single right answer. "You know what you was talking about yesterday? Well, buddy, you're right. Just like you said, except it's even worser."

He leaned toward her, alert as electricity. "What do you mean, Clemmie?"

"What you said. The son of a bitch run out on me. Turned his back and walked away, careless as you please."

"Didn't I tell you?" He was so excited his hands trembled. "I told you. Oxie's a mover, but he's got to moving too fast. Trouble is, he's moving ahead so fast he don't know where he's at. Cut you loose just like that. Didn't I tell you?"

"Oh shut up. It don't do no good to talk about it." His enthusiasm depressed her.

"But what about me, then? You ought to think about it. I'll take a whole lot better care of you than Oxie ever did. The whole thing was, he was always uptown at the courthouse, plugging in with them guys. He wasn't watching after you like he was supposed to. He didn't know where the action was. That was the whole trouble."

She watched his mouth move, suddenly impressed with what a greedy little bastard Arkie was. He didn't care anything for her, nothing. (Nobody did.) All he was waiting for was Oxie to get out of the way so he could belly himself up to the trough. Made her sick to think about it. She couldn't stand a minute more of it, she was going to get her money and leave town. It was settled.

52

"Well, it don't concern you," she said, "not even a little bit. He's already got something else arranged. That's the worse part."

"What now? . . . How's this?"

"Like I said. He's got this other feller to take over. It don't have nothing to do with you."

"What other feller? Who you talking about?"

—Think fast, Clemmie.

"Well . . . I don't know what his name is, exactly. One of these high-toned-looking johns. He's sort of an old feller. You ain't never seen him."

"Around here?"

"No. Like I was telling you: high-toned. Somebody Oxie knew around the courthouse. He lives somewhere out in Otter Lake, I believe."

She had named one of the most expensive residential districts in Braceboro.

Arkie leaned back into his seat. His face showed utter disbelief. "Oh come off it, Clemmie. What would a guy like that . . . ? You're joking me, ain't you?"

"No I ain't. Not a bit I ain't. An old kind of guy. White hair. Looks like your grandaddy. But he's one of them bad kind, you know? Likes to knock you around. That's how he gets his goodies."

—There. That ought to fix it.

He looked scared. "Oxie told you this?"

"Well no, he didn't tell me who it was, but I could tell from the way he talked about him. I knew exactly who it was."

"How?"

She busied herself making another drink. She didn't want to look at Arkie for fear she'd burst out laughing in his face. She could fake him out like this all night. He wasn't nearly so smart as he thought he was, he wasn't smart at all.

"I happened to run into him one night," she said. "That's how I know. And it wasn't no goddam picnic, I can tell you that. I was black and blue for a week."

—Better and better.

53

"Clemmie, for God's sake . . ."

She risked a peek now. He really looked scared. There was something eating at that boy.

"Clemmie," he said earnestly, "you don't want to have nothing to do with this john, you want to leave him strickly alone. I'm telling you. He's one of these here per-verts. You don't know what he might take a notion to do to you. Somebody like that."

"I ain't worried. That don't bother me at all. Because he ain't going to lay eyes on me. I don't have to put up with no kind of stuff like that."

"What you going to do?"

"I'm getting out of this damn dumb town. Simple as that."

"How? Where you going to? What you going to do?"

She laughed. It raised her spirits to see Arkie so bewildered. He wasn't so damn smart. "I ain't decided yet. Maybe I'll go down to Arkansas, like you're always jibbering about."

"Who's going to stake you?"

"I don't need nobody. Stake my own self. I got some money, don't you worry. Teacher's holding it for me."

"You gave your money to that lush? You're crazier than I thought. Whole lot crazier. There won't be a brownie left, not a cent. You gave him any money he's drunk it up a long time ago."

"That's what you think. I gave him a hunderd dollars to hold for me so that goddam Oxie couldn't get his paws on it. And anytime I want it, all I have to do is go and pick it up."

"Pure craziness," Arkie said. "Wave hello to me from the moon when you get there."

"That's all you know," she said. She finished her drink and screwed the cap on the pint and tucked it back into her clutch bag. All her motions were neat and exact. She felt now that she had planned every inch of her life; everything was going precisely as it should. "I'm going to pick it up right this minute."

"Wave hello, that's all," Arkie said.

And then an hour later she was looking for Arkie once more.

She had discovered anew how sharp he was. He really was smart, he'd called every turn beforehand. She was fairly tight again. She had finished the first pint and sent out for another, and the whiskey was smoldering in her like a partially damped fire. Mostly though she was angry at herself. Stupid, stupid. How could she have been so dumb? Handing over your money to a drunk: you might as well fling it in the city dump and forget about it. No way in this lifetime she could get it back and no satisfaction to be got out of Teacher. She supposed that she could cut his throat, but even that wouldn't make her feel any better. Not the way Teacher was.

She'd finally tracked down the son of a bitch in the Big Bunny; he wasn't in the Starlite or Juanita's or the Champagne. (Where the barkeeps were already giving her the hard eye.) And then when she'd cornered him he started out laying down some horse manure about some friend of his and how he'd been sick himself and laid up. She spotted these lies right off the bat. Hadn't she seen him sitting in the joints every single day of the week, drinking beer and reading those sillyass books? If she'd had the least thought that it was her money the bastard was drinking on he would've had a dry spell that would make Death Valley look like the French Broad River. Not that she'd let him get away with anything. Not hardly. She'd called him every name in the book and then a whole bunch they hadn't learned how to spell yet. She said she was going to get the cops on him. Said she had some razor friends who would stomp his ass into the pavement. By God, she was going to wrap the chair leg around his head her own self.

Finally he'd had to own up. He had spent her money. He'd been drinking on it until there was less than ten dollars left.

And then. And then with everybody in the place gawking at them he busted down crying. Like a snot-nose kid. Busted down crying while she stood there with her hands empty and her face burning.

What was a girl to do?

Somebody like that.

55

What could you do?

. . . Son of a bitch.

Yet . . .

And yet . . .

You could see how maybe it wasn't all his fault. She knew about lushes. God knows, she'd lived with enough of them. They were just that way; if you had any sense you knew better than to stand between a lush and his bottle. They couldn't help themselves, it was a simple fact. . . . She hadn't figured Teacher was that far down, that was all. Must be something made him like that; something she hadn't counted on. It had happened to him a long time ago. She'd bet anything it had been a girl. Some girl had done him dirt and that was the hardest thing for a man to get over. . . . Not that Teacher was much of a man to begin with.

To bust down crying like that.

It made you feel just awful.

Arkie had tagged it from the beginning and all the way down the line. He'd called every turn. You had to give the little bastard credit. It was hard to believe how much he knew about what was going on. Where did he come by it? Of course the way he lived accounted for some of his braininess. He was in a fix where he had to keep working, had to scrabble for every poor inch. But she knew guys like Arkie on Gimlet, on Rance, on Rutherford, on Bunker Street, all plugging away, all scrabbling; but not one of them she knew of who could see two days ahead. It was a gift. It was Nature. Arkie had found the handle.

So once more she was walking Gimlet, up and down, up and down, looking for the little guy. She noticed that the johns on the sidewalk were watching her with amusement but she was past caring. Let them have their little joke. Had they never before seen a lady just a weensy bit tipsy? Hell, most of the world stayed drunk these days.

(She was hoping some jerk would stop her and try to make a pass. By God, she'd let him have it with both barrels.)

————

Arkie didn't make his living by hiding from people. She found him easily enough, in the Champagne Club. She broke into his bowling game, shouldering a stupid-looking gray-haired farmer out of the way.

"Well," she said.

"Well."

"I bet you think you're something smart."

"Did you get your money?"

"I got what there was." She opened her left hand, revealing eight dollars and thirty-five cents, wet with sweat.

"Jesus God. Is that all?"

"That's every bit." She stiffened herself, held her head high. "You had it all figured out, didn't you? I guess you're awful proud of yourself."

He put down two quarters on the machine. Wasn't often you got to see that, Arkie paying a john off.

"Let's go take us a walk," he said.

"I been for a walk. I'm going to have me a drink."

"Wait a minute."

He crossed the room and spoke to the barkeep for a moment and then came back. "Let's go this way," he said. He ushered Clemmie toward the back, steering her lightly by the elbow. She almost told him to keep his damn hands off, but then realized she was rather grateful for the aid. She'd had a bit more than she'd thought.

He took her past the shouting red-faced drinkers and past two tall refrigerated cases with glass fronts in which were stacked beer and milk and soft drinks and flat gray frozen hamburgers. They went beneath four huge ungainly piles of empty beer cartons and entered a small bare room with a square wooden table and eight or nine chairs scattered about.

"Here we go," Arkie said. "I told Roy to bring you a set-up. He'll be along in a minute."

"Good." She giggled.

"How you feeling? You okay?"

57

"Fine and dandy." She sat down suddenly.

Arkie drew up a chair and sat so near that their knees almost touched.

"You look kind of funny."

"Well, you ain't no Rory Calhoun yourself."

"That's pretty tough to take, losing your dump like that. I'll settle with Teacher, don't you worry about that."

"You let him alone," she said fiercely. "Don't you even say nothing to him." Emotions were going through her as quickly as the pictures in a movie: anger, and then a confused tenderness, and then she was washed out, tired and helpless. "It ain't worth it. Just forget about it. . . . Anyhow, I got some money."

"Sure God, you ain't going to let him get away with it."

"Leave him alone, I told you. Teacher can't help what he does. It's all the fault of that damn Oxie anyway."

"It ain't Oxie that bothers me."

She saw Arkie shudder; it crept up his torso and down his arms. Something eating on that boy.

"It's this other john," he said. "This here per-vert. What did you say his name was?"

"Don't know his goddam name."

In fact, she could hardly remember having told the lie.

"Ain't no telling what he might do to you, somebody like that. Them kind of guys, they crazy in the head."

Now she remembered. Ha ha.

"He don't worry me even a little bit. He messes with me, I'll shoot his ass off."

Arkie grinned. "What with? A loaded finger?"

"I got a gun," she said carelessly.

"You got a gun?"

"I even got a bullet for it."

"You really have got a gun?"

Roy, gangly and freckled, pushed open the door and brought in on a tray two glasses, a quart of Seven-Up, and a blue bowl filled with ice cubes. He left without speaking.

58

Clemmie fetched out her virgin pint and opened it. "Let's have us a nice drink," she said. "You don't get to live but one time."

"I'll take some Seven-Up."

He was chewing his lip and rubbing his thumb beneath his jaw. You could tell he was thinking hard. She smiled. Arkie was smarter than anybody gave him credit for. She was interested to see what he would come up with.

"How about loaning me that gun?" he said.

"Good Godamighty."

"How about it?"

"You gone plain crazy, ain't you?"

"No."

"What in the world you want with it?"

"Little something I want to take care of."

Rapid garish images fluttered in her mind. She was thrilled to the marrow.

"Sure God, you ain't going to go up against Oxie. He'll bust you into tiny pieces."

"How come not go up against him? What's he ever done for me?"

"I don't know. But I sure know what he's done for me."

"Anyhow, it ain't him. It's this other john you was telling about. White-headed guy."

"Where you going to get hold of him?"

"Oxie. He'll be hanging around somewheres with Oxie. Court-house maybe. Or maybe down at the jailhouse."

"Oxie'll bust your ass into kindling wood."

"Son of a bitch won't do nothing. Can't. He's got too much to lose." Arkie frowned and uttered a bitter sigh. "It don't seem like I got a thing in the world to lose."

"You've lost your brains, is all."

"That's the way it is, though. I got me a place where I can get away and hide out."

"Where?"

"I got a place."

59

"When you figuring on all this?"

"Anytime, it don't matter. Tonight."

"You've plumb lost your marbles."

He shrugged.

She was burning with excitement and she felt somehow that she was on the verge of a strange and important revelation. She was going to know things she had never known before. The truly momentous event of her life was going to happen and it was . . . Well, it was *fun*. It was a way to get back at Oxie, but even that wasn't the most interesting part. Something big was going to take place and she was going to have a piece of it. Wild horses couldn't stop her.

Hoo.

Clemmie.

She was a live one.

Ignominy of a Skylark

Consider the Skylark Society.

In a flint-tough pragmatic world is there even a tiny niche where idealism may survive?

Or perhaps that is not the real question. Maybe the real question is whether a code of behavior crudely extrapolated from the printed page can find an arena of action in quotidian reality. Maybe it's merely a literary or pedagogic question.

The Society had been in existence for three years. At the beginning it had boasted nine members, but our modern age is one of waning faith, nervous apostasy, and it is filled with distracting enticements toward the unreflective life. So that now the Society membership had dwindled to three.

But let us recognize that at no time had the Skylark Society offered very much in the way of creed or doctrine. Even diversion was limited. In fact, with a couple of dozen cans of beer and two furtive packages of cigarettes the members prepared themselves for a gala evening. When they remembered to. When there wasn't a football game or a basketball or softball game. Or a dance in the high school gym. Or, later on, when there wasn't a James Bond movie in town. Most of the dropouts transformed to unrepentant James Bond devotees.

The Society acquired its name not from Shelley's (hardly!)

gaseous symbol for the poetic visionary, but from the famous spaceship that departed this planet Earth from Washington, D.C., in the early 1930's. The spaceship *Skylark* was powered by a then unknown element appropriately called X. (Which was later identified either as a crude type of atomic propulsion or as a raw form of anti-gravity matter . . . Take your choice.) It was piloted by a clean-cut young scientist named Richard Seaton, the discoverer and developer of X. Upon departure, Seaton carried with him a crew consisting of his own fiancée, Dorothy, his scientific colleague and closest friend, Martin Crane, and his friend's fiancée. The *Skylark* was hotly pursued by Seaton's personal and ideological nemesis, a sinister and coldly logical man named Blackie DuQuesne, who had managed through criminal means to lay his hands on the secret of X.

And this was only the beginning. The first *Skylark,* although a true marvel of theoretical intuition and engineering know-how, was merely a primitive prototype of the later vessels bearing the same name. What you might call an *Ur-Skylark.* (Seaton retained the name out of sentiment.) Each later *Skylark* dwarfed its predecessor in size, speed and technological magnificence. The armament especially kept increasing in grandeur. All the *Skylark*s visited strange planets by the score and there were numberless wild adventures, all incidental to the continuing universal—and rather Manichean—battle between Seaton and DuQuesne.

. . . It was about this kernel of adolescent mythology that the Skylark Society of the city of Braceboro, North Carolina, was formed.

Linn Harper was always indisputably the leader of the Skylark Society. At the commencement this was a necessity since he was the only one of the group who owned the novels by E. E. Smith, Ph.D., in which the *Skylark* adventures were recounted. These were three novels: *The Skylark of Space, Skylark Three* and *Skylark of Valeron.* As juvenile books go, they weren't so bad, except for the complete lack of sexuality; the prose was quaint, stilted and shymaking, but the narrative pace was exciting and the thought was mildly liberal in intention.

Later, E. E. Smith, Ph.D., abandoned this series of stories and embarked upon another detailing the vicissitudes of keeping law and order in a heavily and variously populated universe. In this latter series came *Triplanetary, First Lensman, Galactic Patrol, Second Stage Lensman* and *Children of the Lens*. These books too were beloved by the Skylark Society.

But after a while the Society began to go on to other things. They read Dr. Smith's books so fervently and so often that there came a time when many of the members were rereading solely to heighten their feelings of nostalgia. Which are perhaps the keenest of adolescent feelings, but even these will carry you only so long. Or maybe it's a simple truth that one thing leads to another. At any rate they set out through the clamorous pages of science fiction, reading fairly thoroughly through the works of Clifford D. Simak, L. Ron Hubbard, James Blish, Jack Williamson, John W. Campbell and A. E. Van Vogt.

Here came a cropper. Although Van Vogt's *The World of Null-A* contained sufficiently exciting action, it also had a confusing and generally incomprehensible plot. What the hell was going on? They looked to Linn Harper, their acknowledged leader.

Who, with the infuriating smirk of intellectual superiority, caused them to know that the key to this puzzling novel was tucked away in a work on general semantics called *Science and Sanity*. This volume was bristly with diagrams, serried with statistics, leaden with terminology; and most important it was eight hundred pages long. Heavy. When Benny Warner dropped it with an awesome thud on a coffee table in the basement rumpus room of Linn Harper's house, he fully expected the table to fly apart to sawdust. The mere physical aspect of the book caused an immediate revolt among the rank and file of the Skylarks. Two members fled ingloriously, never again to be glimpsed within these visionary precincts. A third member, although not realizing it at the time (case of shock, perhaps), was dealt a mortal blow. He struggled manfully onward for some seven days, but the bare mention of Berelson and Steiner's *Human Behavior* sufficed to do him in and he was borne from the battlefield on his shield.

Sennet and tucket for a valiant heart.

And now even the enduring remainder became restive. Linn Harper decided that there was no special urgency about their unclear anabasis and for a while he led them along an easier path. They began to read delightedly the work of another science fiction writer of the 1930's, Stanley G. Weinbaum. They liked *The Black Flame* and *Dawn of Flame* and were immediately captivated by a book of stories called *A Martian Odyssey*. When, because of the arguments engendered by this latter material, works of popular astronomy began to be seen around, the faithful did not seriously demur. For there is a rather glamorous attraction in the perfunctory study of physical science. The universe is, after all, a gaudy place in which to live. . . .

And Linn had by now taught himself something of tactical procedure. He deliberated more, became circumspect in his choice of subjects for conversation. He pondered whether to introduce George Gamow's books and weighed the possible distinctions between the difficulties of Bertrand Russell's *ABC of Relativity* and Lincoln Barnett's *The Universe and Dr. Einstein*. Storer's *The Web of Life* was okay; Eiseley's *Darwin's Century* they wouldn't take. It was almost as if he was in enemy country.

The group had reknitted itself and was burrowing happily through the current issues of *Astounding, Galaxy, If,* and the rest of the magazines, when the short stories of Ray Bradbury began to obtrude upon their attention. Here was true doctrinal difficulty. The trouble was, Bradbury wasn't really a writer of science fiction.

Was he? Really?

No. He was against science. He was an anti-science fiction writer.

Anti? Come on. What kind of sense does that make?

True, though.

How can you be anti-science? How can you deliberately turn your back on progress?

But see, that's the whole point. Look at the mess progress has got the world into. How can you call it progress, things like they are?

Well, if he doesn't value progress, what does he value?

He has other values. Literary values. Humanist values.

Oh yeah? What's science then if it's not humanist?

Science is partly humanist, can't deny that. But there's too much exclusion of the emotions. Bradbury is against that. He's sort of like . . . well, Steinbeck maybe. Or somebody.

So they read about in Steinbeck. *Of Mice and Men* they liked best, and because it's probably a simple truth that one thing leads to another they tackled Thomas Wolfe, a local boy whom they had always despised hearing about. (Feeling that he was too much lauded by parents and teachers while *their* favorite authors went ignored.) They understood the sugary wind of Wolfe's rhetoric; it was easy to see where Bradbury got some of *his* stuff. They read Jack London and Hemingway. They read F. Scott Fitzgerald and admitted as a group that they didn't see why he was supposed to be interesting. He was too much like the stuff on the English class reading list, Jane Austen and all that.

But the coup de grâce was Conrad's *Lord Jim.* There was a decisive rout at its advent. That story went round and round and round; you got so you didn't give a damn whether Jim was a coward or not. And the sentences were too long. And it took forever to get started, if indeed it ever did start.

Linn tried to hold the trenches, insisting that the book not only started, but that once you got into it you had a really good story; exciting; gun battles and everything. They listened in utter disbelief.

"Maybe you're right," Benny Warner said. "You've read it and I haven't, But if it's got all that, the least he could do is try to get you interested."

"But," Linn said, "he's got to have all this other stuff at the front so that you'll know what the problem is when you get to the end. If he didn't do it that way, you wouldn't know what the book was about."

"I don't think I care what it's about. I think I'll stick to Heinlein."

"You're missing something really good."

"Maybe so," Benny said. "I wanted a motorbike for my birthday and I didn't get that either."

And so Benny departed, and two other members departed in his company.

Now there were three, counting Linn himself. He considered. Was it time to retreat once more?

No. There were things you couldn't turn back from. *If push comes to shove,* was one of his father's favorite expressions, and it had now come at least to *shove,* if not to *electric prod.* He withdrew Conrad and substituted Kafka, who went over with the others surprisingly well. They were taken with the fantastic surface of his work and were intrigued enough actually to inquire a bit into what the stories were about. Complaints still, of course: *The Metamorphosis,* for example—look how much more quickly Gordon Dickson would have got that story off the ground. But now the complaints began to ring a bit hollow, something of a formality about them.

. . . Already they were far gone, advanced upon the narrow, tortuous, dismaying path of modern literature. From Kafka they came swiftly—though queasily—to Sartre and Camus.

For ours is an age in which, even among the innocents, idealism cannot long endure.

Could they have taken another turning somewhere and finally immersed themselves in the soap-bubble splendor of *The Faerie Queene?*

Entirely unthinkable.

(Alas.)

During the days of its sojourn upon this lonely blue planet

66

Earth, burning like a sunny atom of dust on the farthest rim of its galaxy, the Skylark Society had rewarded its members not only with the gifts of fellowship and mutual intellectual stimulation; it had also broadened their horizons in other interesting ways. They had corresponded, singly and as a group, with other science fiction enthusiasts in fifteen different states and had even written abroad, to England and to the Netherlands, thus contributing in some small measure at least to the cause of international good will. And they had taught themselves a bit about the practical side of literary endeavor, for they had published two issues of a mimeographed journal entitled *Fantasm,* to which they had all contributed material. For instance, Benny Warner, most vocal of the later apostates, had written two odd unrhymed science fiction poems. Probably the majority of his readers (excepting, of course, the Skylarks) never penetrated the acrostic messages of these verses. If you took the first letter of the first line, the second letter of the second, third of the third, and so on, you came out with two thought-provoking imperatives: (A) fuck you buddy (almost an unrhymed sonnet), and (B) screw all Martians (a narrative poem). Benny found this method of composition uncommonly delightful.

It was inevitably Linn Harper who produced the bulk of the material for *Fantasm.* He wrote a searing indictment of nuclear warfare, an exposé of the terrifying dangers of overpopulation; he wrote two short stories, one concerning an explorer whose sand-traversing vehicle crashes through the floor of a Martian desert into the ruins of an ancient temple, the other about the perils of a crew aboard a spaceship whose mission it is to extract certain gas samples from the sun. His chef d'oeuvre he considered a long and awkwardly documented essay that attempted to prove the intervention of an interstellar race in Earth's prehistory. This one was quite ingenious and he felt solidly satisfied about it.

The two issues of *Fantasm* were sent gratis to friends and correspondents of Society members, to other similar clubs and societies, to random outstanding scientists and science fiction writ-

67

ers. These latter were sent with a mixed attitude of careless curiosity and awed suspense. But they received no replies. The remaining copies now gathered dust in Terry Burge's attic.

But the Skylarks did manage to acquire a modicum of local fame. The *Braceboro Citizen* ran a Sunday feature about the society in Section E. The headline read YOUNG SKYLARKS LOOK TO FUTURE. The text of the accompanying story, while it did not meet with their unblemished approval, was filled with unexpected gratifications. It told, with mystifying exaggerations, of some of their achievements and, with a wide hiatus of understanding, of some of their aims. There had, however, appeared a photographer and there they stood, in two photographs. Of the original Society seven had momentarily returned, learning that there was to be a newspaper story. The seven were shown in the first photo grouped around the Harper dining-room table, staring solemnly and glassily at a model rocket ship. Actually, they looked nonplussed. The other photograph was of Linn Harper alone. He sat at his obviously clean desk in his father's swivel chair, grinning and displaying one of the pets of his magazine collection, an issue of *Amazing Stories* for November, 1929. (But the magazine cover had been whited out by the reflection of the flash bulb.)

Most of the newspaper text was, in fact, devoted to Linn. It spoke briefly of his collection of science fiction magazines: "complete files of *Galaxy* and *If* and *F&SF*," he said, "plus many rare older items." And of his scholarly and personal triumphs: "honor student at Zebulon Johns High School, substitute end for the football team, president of the Science Club, vice-president Latin Club, sec.-treas. Junior Democrats," etc. etc. Some space was given to his opinions: "It is certainly necessary that the medical profession should learn about atomic medicine immediately"; "One of the quickest ways to insure world peace is to institute a common language for all people." Etc. etc. etc.

The other members didn't object to Linn's hogging their newspaper publicity. In justice, they could not; Linn *was* the Society, as they admitted; he deserved what he could get.

68

The final meeting—the last one ever to be held—of the Skylark Society was arranged during the school lunch hour on a Friday in early May. It came to light that none of the hard-core three had found anything to do that night and none of them had prospects for dates. They pondered and jabbered and it was at last decided that Terry Burge would pick them up in his precarious old Dodge and that they would spend the night at Terry's parents' weekend lodge up on Fire Creek, nestled into the side of Bowstring Mountain. They would all three get together. They would rustle up stuff to eat and a load of beer. They would have a high old time. It was settled.

When he got home from school Linn dutifully informed his father of the boys' plans for the evening.

"What are you guys up to now?"

His father was a short man with reddish-brown hair and eyebrows a bit darker in color. The eyebrows were heavily shaggy—they looked like well-used toothbrush bristles—and when he asked a question he raised them until they almost mingled with his hairline. His blue-eyed gaze, though quick and darting, was almost ferociously intent. There was about him all in all the impression of animal fierceness, frustrated but not blunted.

"It's nothing special," Linn said. "We just thought we'd spend the night up at the lodge."

"When are you planning to get back?"

"Tomorrow afternoon. We thought we'd have lunch tomorrow up there and then clean the place up."

"That's commendably thoughtful. . . . Have you asked your mother?"

"I thought I'd ask you first."

"Because you know it's easier to get my permission. You ask me and then tell her I said it was all right. Isn't that how you work it?"

He grinned at his father. He had a friendly photogenic grin he relied on a great deal.

"Yes sir."

"Okay. As long as you level with me. Have you got any money left?"

"No sir, not much. Less than a dollar."

"I'll let you have five against next week, but that's all. Will that suit you?"

"That's fine. Thank you."

"You're going to keep clear of trouble, aren't you?"

"Yes sir."

Linn smiled. He was contented. It was easy to get along with his father, you just had to level with him. An unaccustomed fond respect overtook him and he rubbed his neck.

He went into his room and changed into dungarees, tennis sneakers, and pulled on a gray sweat shirt. In the kitchen he made a cold chicken and cheese sandwich and drank half a quart of milk. Then he loafed in the back yard; found his basketball and shot for a while at the goal set over the door of the carport. He returned to his room and fiddled boredly with his homework for a few minutes before snugging into Wells's *Island of Dr. Moreau*.

Terry Burge and Don English showed to pick him up a little after five o'clock. He took them into the living room to greet his parents before leaving.

His father turned away from the television newscast. "You fellows try and keep out of trouble, why don't you?"

"Yes sir."

They went out and climbed into Terry's battered old Dodge.

"Your father's a right guy," Don said. "My old man's hard to get along with sometimes."

"He's all right as long as you're square with him. But if you're not you better look out for a tough time."

They stopped at an ice service store and selected an assortment of not very healthy groceries and a case of beer. Terry drove slowly and carefully in the heavy city traffic and even when they were on the nearly deserted small highway headed north he did

70

not speed or drive recklessly. He explained that it was trouble enough just trying to keep the rattling old heap in the road, without trying to bust the speedway records. They didn't answer; neither Linn nor Don had a car; any transportation suited them.

They went about fifteen miles and then turned left on a jolting graveled road. The car clattered and shuddered and gray dust flew up behind it in a long thick streamer. They were grateful when the road transformed to a set of pressed leaf-strewn tracks and there were no more cars to be seen, only trees. The air was quiet and cool and above the sound of the motor they could hear the wind stirring the leaves and branches of pines.

They pulled up beside the lodge. It was a low four-room building made of river rock. There was a wooden porch which ran the length of the front and the windows were small and square. Eight or nine oak trees stood around it, just now in midspring beginning to shade the house. From nearby came the rush and hubbub of a small pebbly stream.

They got out of the car and stretched. They had not talked much driving out—it was hard to hear over the rattle of the car —and now they were silent altogether. Impressible young men; the thousand hushed sounds of the woods and stream, the coolness, the dark smells of shadow and leaf mold momentarily awed them. They carried the groceries and beer onto the porch and balanced the boxes on the knee-high log railing while Terry searched above the door and the window sills for the key. They kept grinning at each other but for some reason they felt awkward. When Terry found the key he whispered, "Wahoo." And they grinned at each other some more and went in.

It was a classy place. Terry's father was a partner in a savings and loan association; he didn't like his work, and when the weather was warm he came out here whenever he got a chance. There was a large denlike living room with a stone fireplace. Oval braided cotton rugs were spotted about on the gleaming oak flooring. An open doorway at the back of the room gave into a shiny kitchen, as long but not as deep as the living room, and

71

two doors to the left of the front entrance opened into separate bedrooms. The ceiling was open to the pitched roof; overhead, stained rafters which they could leap to and swing on.

They hurried to the kitchen with their boxes and flung open the refrigerator door. They began piling food on the counters and refrigerator shelves. Someone had already opened a package of potato chips.

"Hey Don, you ready for a beer?"

"Lord, how you go on."

"What does that remark pretend to indicate, my lad?"

"I mean, open it and don't just talk about it."

"You think we got enough to eat? It's a long way back to the store."

"Man, this isn't all. There's steaks and stuff in the freezer if we really get hungry. There's a whole turkey. You want to thaw out some steaks? Anybody know how to cook a turkey?"

"Well, first you set fire to the Bosporus . . ."

"Get out of here."

"Give that man two tons of horse manure. And we still won't have him paid back."

"Hey, where's the church key?"

"You got it in your shirt pocket."

"No, *he* has it. What are you doing with that thing?"

"Hey man, you ever go hunting around here? Any deer in these woods?"

"Bang bang. Is that any way to treat our wildlife resources?"

"What do you think? Is it too warm to start a fire?"

"Too warm, got to be too warm. It's May, man. Or is it?"

"Damn if I know. I lose track when school is going on."

"Yes, but a fire's nice anyway."

"Let's stick some wood in. It'll get cooler out here after dark."

"Who's got the opener now?"

"Good Lord, is it lost again?"

Had anyone remembered to bring along a deck of cards?

No.

72

Wait, no sweat. There were three or four decks in the drawer there. . . .

The three of them agreed that this was the way to live, a man ought to spend his life in the woods.

"Give me room, man," Terry said. He pushed them to one side, making a narrow space in the aisle between stove and counter. "Look. Who is this? Tell me who." He gave a not very accurate imitation of their basketball coach's manner of walking. "Tell me who."

"Constipated penguin."

"Ruptured goose. With a sunburn."

Two cords of wood were stacked beneath the eaves behind the cabin. They brought in a couple of armloads and piled them in the fireplace and left a few sticks lying on the hearth. Don English stayed in the kitchen, busily working at their meal. But the dinner never got formally laid because they kept snatching it up as soon as he set it aside. They gobbled fried bologna sandwiches with mayonnaise, gristly hamburgers on dissolving loaf bread with mayonnaise and onion, raw slices of tomato, carrot, and cucumber, cheese and crackers, cheese and potato chips, uncooked bologna and cheese. And they opened new beers, spraying the walls and appliances. They gulped it down.

"Hey. Either of you guys ever date Marjorie Lerner?"

"Good God."

"She's a werewolf. Takes more spare blood than I got to date her."

"Oink oink."

"Listen to the children of the night. What music they make."

"Oh come on. She's not so bad."

"Oink oink."

"What is this? You got a case on her? You better watch yourself."

"Pure pig."

"Well, I'd date her. I'd date her on a bet. I'd do it."

"This guy knows something we don't."

"Sounds like. What? Does she go down?"

"Yeah. Down to the Bi-Rite for a bottle of milk."

They got out the cards and tried poker, nickel ante. The three-handed game wasn't satisfying. They switched to hearts but they were still only three. Finally they took a hunting cap from a hook and began pitching the cards at it.

"Hey Don, did you ever tell Linn what your old man said when he saw your picture in the paper?"

"He didn't tell me. What did he say, man?"

"Ha. He said, ha ha, he said he was glad I was hanging out with some clean-cut young man instead of a gang of hooligans. Clean-cut like that young Harper, he said."

"He was never righter. You hang with me and I'll cut you clean every time."

The fire was blazing and snapping like a western movie gun battle. Waves of heat shuddered in the room.

"What we need is some popcorn to pop."

"I'm going to serve myself. Anybody else want a beer?"

Linn removed his sweat shirt.

"Oh man. Look at that shirt Linn's sporting. Who you trying to make out with, honey?"

"Marjorie Lerner, that's who."

Linn made a face.

"Good God. Oink oink and *oink*."

"Dammit, she's not that bad. Nobody's that bad."

"Good eve-ning. I am Dra-cula."

They gathered up the cards, put them into the box and returned them to the desk. They slumped, screwed their shoulders into the backs of sofa and chairs and settled to drinking. They stretched their legs, farted and belched, talking about Camus's *The Stranger*. They pronounced it Kay-moose.

"No."

"Come on, man. I'm not going to believe it."

"Why not? Can't you see how it would happen? Can't you see some of it in yourself?"

74

"No."

"Look, man, what's he supposed to be driving at? There's his mama lying dead and then he goes out and kills this guy and then he doesn't care. What he says, It's all one to me. I don't believe it. This Camus, he's putting you on."

Linn considered. "It's a gratuitous act." He pronounced the words with extreme care.

"Thank you, Dr. Mud, for explaining everything so clearly."

"What the hell does that mean, a gratuitous act."

"Well. Uh. It means you don't give a damn."

"Yeah. He keeps saying that in the book. But what I say is that you do give a damn. You can't help it."

"But see, that's the point. Even if you do care it doesn't make any difference. No difference whatsoever."

"This guy More-salt . . . I don't believe all that."

"It's true, anyway."

"Could you do that?"

"Do what?"

"What he does. See, man, the fuzz are going to get him. He's a criminal. Could you become a criminal without any reason?"

"Sure I could."

"Oh get off my back. Criminals are people who can't make a living any other way. They're forced into it."

"Yeah. Like in *Les Misérables*." Pronounced as if there was a class of persons not quite so unhappy as another: less miserables.

"The point is that we're all like that to begin with. All of us, criminals without a reason."

"Let's see you do it then."

"Do what?"

"Do that thing. Become a criminal for no reason in the world."

"Sure."

"Not in my lifetime."

"Sure."

"Well, let's see you do it. I'm willing to put up five dollars."

"I want a piece of that action."

"No, wait." Terry rose. Although the heat was nearly unbear-

75

able, he went to the fireplace and added another chunk of wood. "We can't make a bet," he said. "Because that would give him a reason. Ruin the whole idea." He brushed his hands on his pants legs.

"Well," Linn said, "it's still true. Just because I can't prove it doesn't mean it's not true." He had felt odd, queasy, during the latter part of the discussion, and now he was freshly relieved.

"It just means that we don't bet, that's all," Terry said. He sat down again.

"That's all it means," Don said. "We won't bet." He leaned forward. "Tell me, babe, who are you going to kill?"

"Nobody."

"So. See there . . ."

"I couldn't kill anybody. But I could commit a crime."

"You can talk about it. That's all I've seen so far."

He was tipsily and darkly serious. He rose, took off his wristwatch and laid it on the table. He took his billfold from his back pocket and laid it beside the watch. It seemed to him suddenly that he was the lead actor in some incomprehensible play. He wished he knew the rules.

"There," he said.

"There what?"

"My watch has got my initials on it. If I commit a crime and if the police catch me, they won't be able to trace who I am. My folks won't be able to help me out. So. What kind of crime do you want me to commit?"

"Rob the old bank," Don said. "Rob the First National. If you split the take with us we'll promise not to rat to the dirty coppers. Ain't that right, Bugsy?"

"No, man," Terry said. "Can't you get it through your head? It can't involve any money. That would give him a motive."

"No money?"

"As far as what we're talking about goes, money's just chicken feed."

They fell silent for a moment and then Terry said softly, "Of course. That's it."

"What?"

"Chicken feed."

"You want to run through that once more?"

"He doesn't have any reason to steal chicken feed. It's a gratuitous act, all right."

"Where is any to steal?"

"There's a warehouse on the right-hand side of the highway just before you turn off on the gravel road." Terry was talking to Linn now. "You can't miss it. It's a concrete block building with a sign. Spartan Feed Mills or something. All you have to do is go and get it. Get a twenty-five-pound bag."

Don looked at Linn. "I don't know, man. How do you feel about that? Chicken feed . . ."

Linn grinned with what jauntiness he could manage. "Give me the car keys," he said. "I'll be back in an hour."

Terry finally handed them over with, it seemed, some reluctance. "I guess you know what the hell you're doing." It didn't sound like a statement.

"Well," Don said, "if you happen to get into any trouble, give us a ring. We'll vouch for you as Braceboro's leading second-story man and rapist."

"He can't call," Terry said. "This place doesn't have a phone."

Linn had some trouble backing and turning the car in the narrow space by the cabin; he'd never had much driving experience. He drove very slowly on the rocky road. It occurred to him that he was already committing a crime, since he had no driver's license.

When he came to the asphalt highway he turned right, still going very slowly. Whenever he saw the shine of headlights in his rear-view mirror he worried furiously, and when a car came toward him he tried to avert his head so that he wouldn't be recognized. He felt sillier and sillier and guilt was in him already for what he had merely planned to do.

He found it without trouble, but it was a more forbidding place than he'd counted on. A low rectangular block building painted white: it might as well have been a bank or a fortress. He pulled the car over to the side of the dusty parking lot into the shadows dropped from some bushes growing on a cut bank. The only light was a smeared and dappled white light from a streetlamp about twenty-five yards away.

He walked to the front of it and stood looking. There was a huge metal sliding door for loading, clinched at the bottom with a stubbornly thick hasp set in concrete. Over the door was the sign: Spartan Stock Feed Products; in the odd light he couldn't distinguish the colors, they looked merely gray and black. On the right side of the door there were two windows side by side, strongly and narrowly barred with iron. No smaller door. He knew there had to be an office door. Then he noticed a set of low cement steps that led to the space walled off by the big sliding door. The office entrance was inside, he was locked away from it.

Round to the side he went, but here was nothing but a long white wall, blank except for a series of slots where blocks had been left out in the construction. These were air vents; a pygmy couldn't squeeze through them. And the back of the building was simply a mirror image of the front except that there was only one of the barred windows and no steps.

He went to the edge of the parking lot and searched and came back with a hefty stone and began hammering at the padlock on the back door. After a few hard whacks he stopped; the blows resounded booming and echoing from the great slab of metal. It was like beating some huge drum. He could see no houses close by, but he felt certain that the noise could be heard for miles, that he had awakened every peaceful sleeper. And cold sweat came out all along his body. He flung down the stone, tried to think. Now if he were only one of John W. Campbell's Martians he would be able to filter the atoms of his body through the atomic lattice of the block wall. . . . Well yes; but even so he wouldn't be able to get the sack of chicken feed out.

He considered going back to the cabin. No. If he gave up, Terry and Don wouldn't. He'd never live it down. He thought of

78

making up some adventurous wild lie to excuse himself, but he knew he'd never get it by their ruthless cross-examination. No dice. He'd better limber up the old ingenuity. . . .

So he thought that perhaps he could get into the place from the top. First of course he had to get to the top.

When he stepped back from the building he noticed the drainpipes, one at each corner. He went to one of them and grasped it with both hands and shook it, then set his foot against the corner and pulled hard, straining and grunting. So far as he could determine the testing hadn't budged it. So he shot back the sleeves of his sport shirt and spit on his hands and picked up some dust. But when he grabbed the drainpipe again it felt slick and he carefully wiped the dust off on his trousers.

He began climbing. It was hard work. One step out of three his shoes slipped on the painted blocks and he hugged himself fiercely to the galvanized pipe. He was grunting and panting and drenched with sweat. His hands were scraped and burning and his left elbow ran bloody where it had been skinned raw. Worse still, he discovered that he desperately needed to take a leak; his bladder was fiery. Eight cans of beer. Still he persisted, and in a few minutes he was able to take the sharp edge of the roof with one hand. He shifted the other and hung resting for a moment before he scrabbled his feet on the drainpipe and arrived safely. He lay a while face down on the edge to catch his breath.

When he rolled over and stood up—unsteadily—he was keenly disappointed. There was nothing. He had been hoping for a skylight or at least a fire door, but it was only a slightly slanted tarred roof with four dinky tin ventilation chimneys, not more than four inches in diameter. No way. Nothing. He walked up and down for a minute or so and then went again to the back of the building, to the corner opposite the one he planned to climb down. He stood at the very edge and unzipped and began pissing off.

"Hey!" It was a low growly voice from below.

A light slanted and bobbed for a moment and then shot upward. Linn stood urinating in the full stubborn glare of a flash-light.

"Hey buddy. What do you think you're trying to do?"

He giggled. "What does it look like I'm doing?"

"Well, goddammit, you nearly peed on *me*."

"I'm sorry," Linn said. "I didn't know anyone was below."

"Yeah?" A pause. "Cut the water off and come down here. This is the police." The light turned away from him and flashed on the side of the building. "Hey Mack. Here he is. He's up on top of the roof."

Linn finished and came painfully and quickly down the drain-pipe. He didn't know what else to do. The light shone on him all the way down.

When he touched ground his knees were shaking and his hands and forearms were raw. He felt stupid with fright. He tried to face the light but someone grabbed him by his shoulders and spun him about.

"Put your hands out and lean over against the wall. Go on, lean over."

They searched him, patting his sides and pockets and legs with sharp deft slaps, but they took nothing from him.

"Okay. You can stand up now."

He stood straight but kept his back to them. He was afraid tears might come to his eyes.

"All right. What were you doing up on the roof?"

"Nothing, sir . . . Just what you saw."

"That right? That's how you usually take a leak, climb up on a rooftop?"

"No sir."

They paused and he tried to tell from the sound of the voices if they were amused. He couldn't tell.

"Were you trying to break into this warehouse, son?"

"Yes sir." He said it almost without thinking. And after he'd said it he thought that it was right. Since he'd got caught he ought to tell them.

80

A long silence this time. Then: "What do you think, Mack?"

"I think it's time to ride downtown."

"Let's go, son."

The patrol car was parked in front of the building. The headlights were off but the front doors were open; they hadn't slammed them when they came looking for him. The one called Mack got into the driver's seat. The other policeman opened a door and ushered Linn into the back, squeezing his elbow. The back doors had no inside handles and there was a metal grill with diamond-shaped holes between the front and back seats. The policeman who had been questioning Linn looked huge in the small space; he seemed all metal buttons and leather, and he creaked slightly each time he moved. Linn thought that he wasn't really angry; he seemed instead slightly amused and rather puzzled.

"Why were you trying to get into that place? Do you think there's a lot of money in there to rob?"

"No sir."

"What were you looking for then?"

"Chicken feed."

"Uh huh. You're in a bunch of trouble, you know that? You think the smartass answers are going to help you? Is that what you think?"

"No sir."

"You were just trying to pull my leg some, that right?"

"No sir."

"Now what the hell would you be wanting with chicken feed?"

Linn thought. If he told them the whole story they would surely get the names of his friends from him. He couldn't tell them that. Anyway, how could they believe the story, the argument about Camus, all that? He could hardly believe how it had happened himself. Already it seemed to have taken place many years ago. It was part of some other mode of experience, something he himself didn't understand.

"I'd rather not say, sir."

"Why not?"

81

"I'd just rather not say."

"Have you been drinking?"

"No sir. Not really. Few cans of beer. I wasn't drunk."

"You're not one of them dope fiends, are you?"

"Oh no sir."

He chuckled. "You sound surprised I'd ask you. But there's a lot of that going around these days. Young people, good families and all. You'd be surprised."

Then they rode in silence. Linn wasn't so frightened as at first. The policeman beside him seemed to intend him no harm. If anything he seemed pretty easygoing, a stern but tolerant uncle. They had come into town and now under the more frequent streetlamps Linn tried to form a better impression of his companion. He had ragged blondish hair poking out beneath the edges of his cap. His face was large and round. A florid complexion. On his prominent nose were conspicuous red and blue veins. Like an uncle who spent his evenings drinking blended whiskey at the kitchen table and listening to the Senators play ball on his small clock radio.

When the car pulled into the lot beside the police station he leaned toward Linn and said in a soft thick confidential voice, "Now son, you're not going to give us any trouble, are you? You're not going to try to run when we get out here, are you?"

"No sir."

He nodded. "That's good, that's right. You're too smart for that kind of stuff, aren't you?"

"Yes sir."

But when they got out Linn felt himself grasped by his belt at his lower spine and summarily propelled across the lot and up the steps and through the white worn doors. He thought it a useless insult. Hadn't he just given his word? He stumbled and lurched at the threshold and the one called Mack said, "Watch your step." A thin acid voice. They went down a long corridor with doors opening into clerical offices flanked with large panes of dark frosted glass. The corridor widened into a square space

82

rawly lit by fluorescent lights. They pushed him through the gate of a low wooden railing and halted before a scarred desk loaded down with stacks of papers, papers scattered seemingly at random. Behind the desk sat a paunchy gray man with white hair. He was wearing a police uniform, but the jacket hung on a coatrack over next to a set of filing cabinets. He was eating a candy bar, chewing very slowly.

He gazed dreamily at Linn, standing numbly beside the desk. "What's this one?" he said.

Mack answered. "We found him on top of the Spartan Feed warehouse. He told us he was trying to break in."

He grinned a chocolate grin, speaking to Linn. "You admitted to the officers that you were attempting to break and enter?"

"Yes sir."

"Huh. That's a mighty serious charge, breaking and entering. How old are you?"

"Seventeen, sir."

"Well, let's have a look at your driver's license."

"I don't have one."

"Huh. What sort of identification do you have?"

"I don't have any, sir."

"None at all?"

"I don't have it with me."

"What's your name?"

"I'd rather not say, sir, if you don't mind."

The gray man laughed. Though he'd licked his lips the under edges were still stained with chocolate. "Uh. *I* don't mind." He shifted heavily in his chair and casually wadded the candy wrapper and dropped it on the floor. "But I would've thought you were smarter than that." He began messing with papers. "All right, if that's the way it is." He told the policemen, "Put him in the waiting room."

They took him behind the desk and around a corner to a small bare room without windows. Two benches were against opposite walls. Mack gestured at one of them. "Sit down," he said.

83

"Make yourself comfortable." When they went out they closed the white glassless door, but Linn heard no sound of locking.

He sat. There was nothing to do. He was not now so thoroughly frightened for himself; he was instead keenly ashamed. He just felt very silly. The argument with his friends had been silly, and then accepting that stupid challenge was even sillier. Worst of all, he'd proved himself powerless. He'd taken pride in his intelligence, had in fact vaunted it, and his friends accepted all this quite readily, and then his picture had appeared in the newspaper. Yet for all his reputation for brains he'd been unable to steal twenty-five pounds of chicken feed.

Well, you didn't have to search very hard for the moral of this story.

For a long time he sat leaning forward with his elbows on his knees. When his left thigh began to feel numb he tried slumping with his back against the wall. That was no good either. The bench was too narrow. He imagined that it had been designed purposely to be uncomfortable, a form of mild torture. He tried to reason out why he wouldn't tell the policemen his name. Partly of course it was his friends, he couldn't betray them. And he had the feeling that if he once gave out that information he would inevitably tell everything. . . . But then what had Don and Terry done? Nothing. Nothing against the law, certainly . . . Probably he was just compounding his silliness.

Sooner or later he would have to tell them. Sooner or later his parents would have to find out. He quailed at the thought: not because of the punishment, whatever it might be, but because he had betrayed them. —Just this afternoon, for example, he'd asked his father's permission to go to the lodge with his friends. His father had been, well, very *nice* about it. He'd asked only that Linn keep out of trouble. People often thought of his father as fierce and bitter, an angry man. But he wasn't, not at all. He had certain ideas and he would stick up for them, but if you knew him you found that he was actually a gentle person. Tired, irascible. But never bitter. —And now how could his father help looking upon the trouble Linn was in as anything but evidence of ingratitude? Or maybe he would think that Linn actively disliked him and was trying to embarrass him. He realized for the first time that he and his father had never really made clear their feelings about each other.

Suppose his father took it as a purposeful betrayal. That would be the worst. Absolutely.

How long had he been waiting?

Hours and hours.

No. Probably it was only a few minutes. He remembered a science fiction story about a space pilot. For some reason all the chronometers had gone haywire and there was no way for the guy to tell time. He had then devised an extremely complex way of telling time psychologically and it worked out that after six months on his time scale he had become mad. At the end of the story it was revealed that only four days had elapsed in actual time.

He rebuked himself. It was another form of very mild torture.

The door opened and a policeman he hadn't seen before stepped into the room. He was tall and thin, rather young. "Come on," he said loudly. "Sergeant Gaffin wants to see you." He led him back to the desk.

The sergeant was scribbling with a ballpoint pen, bearing down heavily so that the writing came out dark streaks. He didn't look up for a minute or so. When he did he seemed almost surprised to find Linn there. He looked abstracted. Finally he pointed to the candy wrapper he had dropped earlier.

"Huh," he said. "You see that litter on the floor there? Pick it up."

Linn went round the desk and picked it up.

"Now put that litter in the wastebasket."

He did it.

"You see," said the gray man, "litter is ugly. It's ugly and it ain't healthy and it costs the taxpayers money. Don't ever throw litter around in public places."

85

"Yes sir."

"All right. Take him back to the waiting room."

They started round the corner again, the policeman following him.

"Wait a minute."

They halted.

"Son, you don't happen to of remembered what your name is, have you?"

Linn smiled wanly, in case it was a joke. "No sir. Not yet."

"Huh. Well, take him on back."

This time the room looked even more barren than it had before. He gazed wearily at the narrow bench. Now he would like to lie on it, but he was obscurely afraid. They had told him to sit and he supposed that he must sit. But besides fear an edge of anger was beginning to show in him. They were merely trying to demonstrate that they were in control and that they were handling him with extreme gentleness. Foo. They didn't have to show him. He'd read the books, Nelson Algren, Raymond Chandler—those guys. He'd read Richard Wright too. He wouldn't be treated so gently if he were Negro. If the cop who had picked him up had seemed like an uncle, well, all the uncles he knew hated niggers. . . . But why, seeing that they didn't know who he was, were they treating him so well?

He thought about it for a while and then gave up. He had fouled it up properly, he'd made his whole life a permanent mess. He was going to have a police record. He didn't know how the charge would read, attempted felony or some such, he supposed. But it would almost certainly bar him from any decent university. There in one foolish moment had shipwrecked all his visions of becoming a famous nuclear physicist or biochemist. Or a feted science fiction writer. Misery overtook him completely.

Worse—or at least more immediate—was having to face his father. He could postpone it for a while by not identifying himself, but sooner or later . . .

And then there was his mother.

86

Ow.

He simply refused to think about that.

Later they brought him out and took him round to the desk again.

Sergeant Gaffin pointed to a chair, a heavy oak piece with smooth curved arms which was set against the wall. "Pull up a chair and have a sit-down."

Awkwardly he carried it over and placed it at the corner of the desk and sat.

"Son, I forgot how old you said you were. You don't mind telling me that, do you?"

"No sir. I'm seventeen."

"Huh. I would of thought you were some younger. You still in school?"

"Yes sir."

"How's your marks? Pretty good?"

"Yes sir."

He nodded. "I thought when I first seen you you might be a pretty good scholar. . . . You ever been in trouble like this before?"

"No sir."

"Well, I didn't think you had, but it seems to me your face is kind of familiar. Wonder where I might have seen you?"

"I don't know, sir."

"Huh." He rubbed his nose. "I guess it don't make a hell of a lot of difference. . . . Let me get it straight now: you admitted to the officers that you were attempting to break and enter?"

"Yes sir."

"That's a serious crime. You're in a mite more trouble than you probably think you are." He leaned back in his swivel chair and clasped his hands behind his head. "You know, I been hearing nothing but ball-face lies so long I don't hardly know what to think about the truth. We get fellers in here all the time caught out in some little old petty larceny. They don't do nothing but whine and twist and blubber. And then at the end of it they'll

87

come out with some horseshit story about how they've got a hungry sister at home. Or a starving mother. Or a starving wife and kids. They say that because they can't think of nothing better to say. You understand what I mean?"

"Yes sir. I think so."

The sergeant leaned forward and propped his elbows in the litter of papers. "Tell me, son, have you got a flock of starving chickens at home?"

"No sir."

"But you're going to keep on wanting us to believe you were trying to steal chicken feed."

"It's the truth."

"Huh."

Sergeant Gaffin sighed heavily and opened a top drawer and produced a battered package of Winstons. He held it out.

"No thank you, sir. I don't smoke."

He grunted and fished one out for himself. The top of the package split when he stuffed his thick fingers into it. "I wish to hell I'd never started. I believe I could just about give it up if it wasn't for this here job." He lit it and looked wearily at the paper match before tossing it on the floor. "Reason you won't give us your name, you don't want your folks to find out. Ain't that the way it is?"

"Yes sir."

"I guess they'll lay into you hot and heavy when they find out."

"No sir. They wouldn't hit me, but they'd be awfully—"

"Pissed off."

"No. They'd just be sad."

"Okay." He rubbed his blue tired-looking eyes. "It ain't hard to tell you come from a good family. Your teeth and your fingernails tell me that much. And that shirt. You're just damn lucky and you don't appreciate what a good deal you've got. Maybe you don't know enough to. But surely to God you've got sense enough to know that sooner or later you're going to have to tell us who you are. Why don't you just tell us now and get it over with?"

88

"I'd rather not, sir."

"It would make it a whole lot easier on us and on you too."

"I'd rather not say right now."

"You want to gain a little time so you can figure out a good lie to tell them. Ain't that right?"

"No sir. I won't lie to them."

The gray man appeared to consider this answer. Then he nodded, cigarette smoke pouring out his nostrils. Regretful gray clouds of smoke hung about the desk. "Well, son, you don't hardly give me any choice. I'm going to have to put you in the tank. You ain't going to like it, I can fairly promise you that. But like I say, you ain't giving me a choice." He gestured at Linn's waist. "Let's see what you've got in your pockets."

It wasn't much: a little less than two dollars in change, a black plastic pocket comb, a clean handkerchief. He gave the comb and handkerchief back to Linn. "You should of thought to bring along a toothbrush," he said. He gathered the money and sealed it in a manila envelope. "You get this back," he explained. "Only reason we keep it is so the other prisoners won't take it from you."

Linn's palms became damp. That word *prisoner* had an unsuspected weight.

"I guess that's all," Sergeant Gaffin said. "Is there anything I can do for you before you go in?"

"Could you tell me what time it is?"

He shook his head and smiled for the first time. "I reckon not. You got a little secret, I got a little secret." He pushed a button on his intercom and a young policeman entered almost immediately. "Take him on up," the sergeant said.

But as they started away he stopped them. "Wait. I'm supposed to have your belt too."

Linn took it off and gave it to him.

He sealed it in another envelope. "Okay." He waved them on.

Stopped them once again.

"Hold on," he said. "You remember what I told you about litter, don't you? How it's ugly and unhealthy and all. Well, that's

89

litter too." He was pointing to the paper match he had tossed on the floor. "Pick it up and put it where it belongs. . . . Litter don't have to be something big. Get enough little old trash together and it amounts up."

Linn dropped it carefully into the wastebasket.

Then they departed. They went back down the long corridor, but turned right this time and climbed a flight of stairs. The wooden steps were creaky, dark with oil and dirt except in the middle where they were worn white. The edges were white too and scraped away in the center. Beltless, his blue jeans kept slipping and Linn kept hitching them up. It shamed him to do it.

At the second landing they stopped at a metal door and the young policeman rapped with a metal ballpoint pen on a plate set at eye level. In a moment it slid back and a pair of dark brown eyes gazed out.

"One for the tank," said the young policeman.

The door opened and they entered a small anteroom, brightly —almost glaringly—lit. The man who opened the door was in full uniform except for his hat, and he wore a big pistol. Here was another desk, much smaller than Sergeant Gaffin's. The man behind it was unarmed except for a ballpoint pen and a pad of yellow legal-size paper. When they stopped before his desk he barely glanced at Linn.

"Name?"

"I'd rather not say, sir."

He looked up, not at Linn, but at the young policeman who accompanied him. The young man smiled faintly and shrugged.

The man at the desk shrugged too. He looked at his watch and began printing on his pad in large clumsy capital letters. Upside down, but Linn could read them.

11:20. UNIDENT. WHITE TEEN. DARK HR. MED. HT.

"Okay." An utterly bored voice.

The uniformed policeman unlocked another metal door on the other side of the room and ushered them through. He came through himself and locked the door behind him, turning a key in a small circular lock, and then slipping the key with its leather tab into his pants pocket. Linn blinked his eyes rapidly because of the difference in lighting. Now they were in a huge room with whitewashed cement block walls. The south wall, on Linn's left, had three regularly spaced barred windows. The cement floor sloped smoothly around a rather large drain capped with a heavy wire grating. The floor was wet. To Linn's right was a wall of gray steel bars set four inches apart. The three of them, the policemen and himself, were in a corner of a long aisle formed by the outside wall and the wall of bars. Behind these bars was a row of narrow cells set back about twelve feet so that there was another long aisle inside. Six wooden benches were ranked in the interior aisle, steel legs set into the floor. Eight or nine men sat glumly on these benches. One or two glanced up as they came in, but most of them stared at the floor or the walls.

The policeman with all the keys opened a door in the wall of bars and they nudged him through. He locked him in and the two of them went out without speaking.

Linn stood by the barred door a moment, confused by the eerie silence. Since entering this room he had heard nothing but the clank and clatter of metal, the scraping of shoe soles on cement.

The aisle and cells were lit by naked 150-watt bulbs and in this whitish-yellow light Linn felt as helpless as if he were naked. He took the example of the inmates and, keeping his eyes steadily on the floor, crossed and went into the cell immediately in front of him. It was so narrow that the low ceiling seemed to rise when he entered. On the right wall was a sheet of iron suspended horizontally by two chains. The edges were turned up—it looked like a huge cafeteria tray—and a small hole had been bored near the center. The iron sheet and the chain had been painted with silver paint. He could distinguish now the odors of ammoniac disinfectant and urine and still another smell, sweet-sour, thick, musky and greasy. There was a barred window in the north wall, so small it was not much more than a slot, and he crossed and looked out. Not much to see. Across the street that ran behind the police parking lot was a row of grimy brick buildings, warehouses and repair garages. The lot itself looked farther beneath him than he knew it was. There were five empty patrol cars and no policemen about. An empty wax paper cup scudded and halted and then began rolling as the breeze caught it, a breeze that Linn felt no breath of.

That's litter, he thought involuntarily. It's ugly and dirty and it costs the taxpayers money.

From some blocks away he heard the solid clanging thud of boxcars coupling.

Mostly obscured by the parking lot lights, the stars shone above, dim stars like specks of salt.

He turned from the window and lay down on the iron bed. It was invented to be uncomfortable. He tried every kind of position, finally squirmed about and put his left hand beneath his cheek and turned to the wall. But there was no place for his shoulder blade. An inch away was an important message penciled clumsily on the wall: *fuck all son of bitch fuzz*. His shoulder blade began to hurt and he turned on his back and closed his eyes, but the bare light shone red through his eyelids. He felt absolutely helpless, lying like this; it was as if he were waiting for a cruel surgery. A hard sour distaste for himself sprang in him. He had been stupid and he had been silly, which was worse than stupid. When he pondered his present situation he found it impossible to believe. This wasn't his way of life, people weren't supposed to treat him like this. It came to him with the force of revelation: he didn't live like this, he had never even imagined the possibility of living like this.

How then had he dared to pride himself on his imagination?

He tried to think how he was going to justify himself to his father, and he composed several differing daydreams. In one of them his father was stern, immovable, unforgiving, harsh: very Old Testament, very Victorian. In another vision he was calm and affable, pleasant, understanding and ridiculous. In yet another daydream he appeared as weeping, filled with outraged injury, and rather feminine: one of Dostoevsky's tortured souls. All these figures were equally silly. He had no way of knowing how his father would react. He felt that he knew his father well

enough, better than anyone else he knew of that puzzling generation, but when he tried to predict it seemed that he finally did
not know him. Let's see. He was aware that many people thought
of his father as an angry and reckless man. But did they catch
the acid air of disappointment and frustration that hung about
him like an obscuring cloak? There was an attitude of suffering
hope about his father, but it was in no manner a passive suffering. He was a driven man, but driven to himself mostly. And it
wasn't that he was selfish, for he was watchful and caring toward
his wife and toward Linn. It was almost an abstracted regard,
though, as if he was always really thinking of something else.

Linn sighed. Trying to ponder the imponderable. He laid his
forearm over his eyes to keep out some of the light, but this
too was an uncomfortable position.

Helplessly he fell into another daydream, a memory. Not far
from his house was a pleasant grassy hill. In the green summer-
time he went there often, carrying a book or a magazine to read
as he stretched out oblivious on the slope. But then as often as not
he would forget to read, staring and staring into the plumbless
blue sky, or watching the massed clouds, like great snowy heaps
of mashed potatoes, ponderously marching, dropping gulfs of
moving shadow. The sweet heat immersed his body and then,
closing his eyes, he would abandon himself to sensation until the
inevitable sexual fantasies edged into his mind. Then he forced
himself to open his eyes and to try to think through some fanciful
intellectual problem. Or he would turn earnestly to his book,
nibbling a hot and bitter plantain stem. In the grove above he
could hear the metallic scraping cries of blue jays or the barking
of a squirrel, a sound like a windowpane rattling. Or if a breeze
moved through the dark stand of oaks there was a noise like
great sheets of newspaper being spread.

He was rudely jerked away from this memory.

"Hey buddy, wake up. Wake up, goddammit." A voice gritty
and abrasive. Like a rusty hinge.

"What is it?"

He opened his eyes. Twelve inches away a large splotched

face loomed over his own. Dazed confusing blue eyes set into puffy folds of cheek, crudely greased red hair slicked back and a red stubble spread over the face. This face came closer. Whiskey and other smells stained the man's breath.

"Are you awake yet? Wake up. You got to help me out."

"No I don't," Linn said. His tone was curt.

The red-haired man stepped back away from him. He was a hefty little man wearing dungarees—beltless like Linn's—and high-topped brogans. A faded blue work shirt was ripped open all down the front, showing a tobacco-colored noisome undershirt. His manner was defensive. He held his hands flat by his sides.

"Wait a minute," he said. "I wasn't meaning no trouble. I guess maybe I got the wrong guy."

"What do you want?"

He slouched closer; disastrously close, Linn felt. "Buddy, you got to help me out. They're going to get me."

"Who is?"

"Them guys out there." He pointed with his head to the open cell door.

"What are they going to do?"

He opened his eyes wide, seemingly surprised by the question. "Why hell," he said, "they're going to kill me." Saliva dribbled from the corner of his mouth and he rubbed it off on the shoulder of his shirt.

Linn sat up, put his feet on the floor. "No they're not. Nobody's going to hurt you in here."

"That's all you know."

Suddenly he turned his head and vomited. A large stinking splotch of yellowish matter spattered on the cement floor. The man tugged up his shirt front and wiped his mouth and chin, not very efficiently.

Then he went on speaking as if nothing had happened. "Damn right they going to kill me. They got knives and hammers and all. Sneaked them in."

94

Linn got up and, skirting carefully round the mess, looked out the door. So far as he could tell none of the men had moved since the time he had first seen them. "They're not going to bother you. Everybody is just sitting still."

But when he turned around the red-haired man was lying on the sheet of iron, grinning at him. His teeth were the color of creamed coffee and two of them were missing.

"Ha ha," he said. "I got your bed. I've got the old bed now and if you want it back you'll by God have to fight me for it."

"You can have it," Linn said.

He went out and entered the adjoining cell. It was identical to the one he had just left except that there was no window. He sat down on the iron bed and rubbed his face and massaged his neck. He was surprised to discover that he hadn't been frightened of the man. What he most wished for now was the ability not to think, he wanted to stop the desperate drumming of thought and impression. He lay down and once more closed his eyes. Images dropped rapidly through his mind like a house of cards falling.

He lay in silent disgust for a while. Then he felt something tugging at his foot. He looked and saw the red-haired man. He was on his knees at the end of the bed, pulling at one of Linn's tennis sneakers. When he saw him watching he grinned, baring the ugly teeth. "Ah hell," he said. "I thought I could steal your shoe while you was asleep. Just for the joke of it. Be a good joke. You wouldn't know what had happened to it."

"Why don't you just leave me alone?"

The man stood up. "Come on, buddy. Don't be like that. I need to talk to you. I got to. I'm in trouble pretty bad."

"I'm in trouble too," Linn said. "We're all in trouble or we wouldn't be in here."

He reflected that his remark was perhaps unfeeling.

All right, he didn't feel especially charitable right now.

"Don't be like that. You don't know how it is with me. You don't know nothing about it. I got to get out of here so I can go to my sister's funeral tomorrow. She lives way down in Columbia,

95

South Carolina. That's why I got to get out of here tonight. These goddam cops won't pay me no mind, they don't listen to a word I say. You got to talk to them for me and get them to let me out of here."

"They won't pay me any attention. I'm here the same as you."

"They don't know you so good. They'll probly take your word for it. I ain't never seen you in here before. Do this thing for me, buddy. Do this thing for me and I'll give you a straight tip."

"What kind of straight tip?"

The man gave him a greasy fluttery wink. "I know where there's a pretty good-looking old gal over on Flint Street. Man, she'd be plumb tickled to see a fine young feller like you. She'll treat you right. I mean right, buddy." He slid across the bed and clamped Linn's knee with a dirty hand. "You know what I mean, don't you, honey?"

Linn glanced down at the hand, took it by the wrist and lifted it firmly off his leg. He still had no fear. He got up without haste and walked to the cell door. "Just keep away from me," he said. "Just leave me alone."

He went out and took a seat on the nearest bench.

Sitting slumped at the other end was a small wiry man whom he judged to be about forty years old. He was dark complected and had shaggy black hair. When Linn sat down he gave him a steady brown-eyed stare before speaking.

"You got a cigarette, kid?"

"No sir."

The man kept staring at him. There were wide black circles under his eyes and the black eyebrows met in a bristly stripe over his nose. The bare overhead bulb was reflected in yellow dots on his pupils. "That goddam alky fairy been after you?"

"Yes. A little."

"Maybe you should've took him up," he said. "You sure as hell ain't going to do any better than that in here." He gave Linn a long last sorrowing glance and once more began staring at the floor.

Linn stared down too. He unbuttoned his shirt sleeve and rolled it up over his elbow. He observed with clinical detachment that a nervous tic caused a muscle of his forearm to twitch repeatedly. It was a comfortless sight. And though it was cool and the air was damp—the dampness seeming to rise from the wet floor—he felt drops of sweat slide hesitatingly down his sides from his armpits. It was nerves, that was all. He'd proved—to his own satisfaction, at least—that it wasn't physical fear, or not an overwhelming physical fear. Perhaps it was a subtler despair, the same kind of despair that seemed to penetrate the dark man, his benchmate. A notion was fermenting in him, acquiring convincing force. He was beginning to imagine his life in new terms. Why, after all, should he not be here in the tank with the rest of them? This too was a viable mode of life. There was no mistake. Now it seemed logical that he could spend the rest of his years in and out of jails. He wiped his wet palms on his thighs. Actually, once you accepted the idea, there was something exhilarating about it. It was a new idea of freedom.

The red-haired man had come out of the cell. He winked at Linn again, a sanguine garish wink somehow reminiscent of a neon beer sign, and went to the dark man at the end of the bench. When he spoke his voice had become a querulous falsetto, lifting with phony gaiety. Even Linn could tell it meant trouble.

"Why Frankie," he said, "what you doing in here? I thought you was too well covered to ever land in here. Something happen to go wrong? Must of messed up a little, huh?"

"Shut your goddam mouth and keep the hell away from me," Frankie said.

"Come on, Frankie old buddy. What's the trouble? Old Freene Sluder ain't let you down, has he? Why, he's supposed to always take real good care of his drivers. Wouldn't be he's cut you loose, would it? Old Freene?"

"I ain't going to tell you another time." Frankie's voice was sharp and bitter.

"Don't be like that, Frankie. We're old buddies, me and you. If

97

Freene has went and cut you loose you know it don't make no difference to—"

Frankie grabbed a handful of the slick red hair with his left hand and yanked the stammering face down savagely. He gave the fellow two quick blows on the mouth with the heel of his palm. Then he stood up, shifting his grip to take hold of the other by the back of the head. He was much taller than Linn had thought. With the yellow light on his shoulders he looked towering. He grabbed the man again by his right hip. He was still stammering, still trying to talk, but his lips bubbled with blood and spit was smeared on his chin. Frankie tumbled him backward. His shin tangled in the bench leg and he went careening. He fell, helplessly milling his arms, onto a white-haired man sitting on the next bench. This man shoved him off and he landed on the floor and lay there, not trying to get up.

The white-haired man stood. He spoke to Frankie.

"Watch out what the fuck you're doing," he said.

Frankie didn't answer. He leaped over the bench and began to beat him about the neck and shoulders. The white-haired guy kept ducking and slamming away at Frankie's ribs and belly. They fought fiercely, gulping for breath as if they were drowning, their feet unmoving, the force of their blows delivered from swaying torsos. It was hard to tell if either of them was inflicting any real hurt. But their faces were strained and scarlet, the neck tendons stood out like stretched twine and when blows landed on the scalp tufts of hair stood up, irregular spiky horns.

All the other men stood around them in an uneven ring. They started shouldering each other and then restlessly shoving. Presently earnest fighting broke out among them, moiling and clumsy. Loud shouts and squeals and curses rang in the stone and iron room.

The red-haired man scooted across the floor and sat with his back to the wall, well out of the way of conflict. He gazed at the commotion with an expression of simple delight, as a child might look upon a crayon drawing he has just completed.

Two policemen entered the long aisle outside the bars. One of them went down to the far corner and took up the business end of a green plastic garden hose. He was in no hurry, stepping a few yards behind out of the tangle to turn on a worn brass spigot. When the water came through he began playing the lackadaisical stream on the men in the cell. For a moment or two they seemed not to notice; and then the shouting and squealing got louder. When they saw what it was, the noise turned into a sour muttered grumbling and they broke apart, stumbling back to take their accustomed places on the benches. They were soaked entirely and as they sat hunched and huddled there they looked like miserable wet birds.

"All right, that's enough. Turn it off," one of the men said.

But he kept pouring it through.

"Wheeler, goddammit, that's enough."

They were all shouting again.

The policeman noticed Linn, who had stood by a cell door watching all through the melee. He flicked the hose toward him, wetting only the cuffs of his trousers legs, before he went to the faucet and turned off the water.

The policeman standing by the door to the tank said, "All right now, simmer down." He rattled the bars with his nightstick. "Simmer down in there. Let's keep it quiet."

Linn was disgusted. Wet tennis shoes: that was the last straw.

As it got later the tank got crowded. More and more men came in, silent, angry and stumbling.

One of them was a short man, dressed rather expensively in a dark gray suit with a handkerchief, TV fold, edging out of the breast pocket. He wore a blue silk tie and he was sober. He looked to be about sixty years old and had silver hair. His dark hat was pulled straight over his brow. Dark glasses hid his eyes and he kept rubbing his hands together. They were dry as poker chips. "Simply terrible. They have accused me of molesting a child. That couldn't be. I'm sixty-eight years old. I'm a grand-

99

father. I have two wonderful grandchildren, two little girls. It's a terrible mistake. It's not just."

He went into one of the cells and lay down on the bed. There was a man sleeping on his back in the next cell. Linn watched him through the bars. His mouth was open and a stream of discolored saliva crawled down the corner of his cheek. Linn turned away and stuck his head over the bed to stare at the floor. What time was it? Maybe he'd never know, ever. He turned on his back and closed his eyes. Sergeant Gaffin had been right. He didn't like it in here. No no no . . .

But he hadn't broken, he was still constant in his resolve not to tell them his name. Maybe he was even more determined now than before. He still hadn't thought things out, he had formulated no plan. It was imperative that he have a plan.

He wished he could go to sleep. To occupy his mind he tried to remember important information: the distance from the earth to Altair, the names of the twelve moons of Jupiter, the position of the Trojan asteroids in relation to Uranus in March.

And when at last he did fall asleep he dreamed that he was zipping through the cosmos in pursuit of his nemesis, Blackie Du-Quesne. He would mete out justice to him. . . . But in the vision of the stars streaking blindingly by and the comforting glow of the ship's control panel were mixed other images, unrelated, discordant and dismaying.

Oxie

In the fond glass Oxie considers himself. Rapidly he wiggles two fingers of his right hand, twittering a pair of tiny curved scissors. Then he leans to the mirror, passionate but deliberate, and clips at his moustache. He has the fierce bright eye of a bird and he cocks his head like a robin. But it's obvious that he's never going to be entirely satisfied with his moustache. He peers closely, cuts a bit more. He ruminates. This is the best part of his day—not that you could get him to admit it; perhaps he's not even aware of it—here before the mirror, deferentially pampering his face.

Is it simple narcissism? Or is he in love? —But if you asked him Oxie would tell you quite seriously that appearance is important, that good grooming counts, that you should put your best foot forward.

Don't ask him.

Now that the rich black moustache had received its proper attention, he took a cigar from the breast pocket of his dressing gown and lit it with a lighter given him by a sentimental lady. (The only thing she ever gave him that worked . . . Lord, she'd been a weepy bitch.) He lathered his cheeks and began to shave, pulling his skin balloon-tight under the blade. Now and again he laid the cigar on a small glass table and tapped the soft ash into the bathtub, still wet from his daily hot-and-cold shower. When he had finished shaving he rubbed in a citrus-smelling English lotion and went out, leaving the lavatory and tub streaked with lather, hair and ash. He liked to leave a mess behind him in his apartment; it served to remind him that at ten o'clock a maid would be in to clean up, to make a pristine order that he could once again destroy. When he thought about the maid he felt safe, reassured; and that feeling of security was what Oxie had most trouble coming by. His carefully resplendent appearance, for example, was for him no luxury but grinding necessity. He was convinced that once you began to slide, a sock with a hole in the toe or a bad trim around the ears or a collar button not hidden behind the tie knot, Gimlet Street yawned wider to receive you, you could feel that asphalt breath. Help, help. A man could work his way up from Gimlet Street once in his life but he could never do it twice. Because landing down there again would mean that the Thing had broken in him, and when the Thing was broken it could never be wholly mended. A man would have to fall and fall; he could never return to clean streets.

He went into the bedroom to dress. He shrugged out of the dressing gown and tossed it unthinkingly across the crumpled form that lay sleeping under the bedclothes. One more expensive woman in the bed, another necessary luxury, another reinforcement against the icy abysses of the past and the future. Perhaps Oxie might even have admitted, in a moment of unwonted honesty, that sometimes he had to force himself to make love to the women simply in order to be able to find them there in the mornings. Sometimes, if it had been possible, he would gratefully have paid them to sleep quietly next to him while he lay awake, pondering luxuriously in the deep hours of the night. But, alas, the game wasn't played that way. You had to put yourself out for them. The women represented not so much investment of money as of time. He had to woo them, and there went hours of the evening that were already too short. And there were further

102

investments, in manners and in grammar, and Oxie had already frayed both rather badly through assiduous practice.

He set out new linen and spent some time choosing his clothing, finally deciding upon dark green socks, a shirt so white it almost shimmered, dark brown gabardine slacks. Let's see now. He liked his new soft moleskin jacket, but which tie would go with it? At last he chose a dim green suede tie—imported from Rome, the label proclaimed. He laid everything neatly at the foot of the bed. Then he closed the mirrored closet doors and, naked, once more considered himself with true critical attention. —Not too bad, old man. Not bad at all.

The olive skin was not wrinkled anywhere yet, and the muscles of the arms and shoulders and neck still retained tone and smoothness. It was almost a swimmer's body. He was still strong, especially in the neck and shoulders where he was so deceptively strong. That was how he'd got his Gimlet Street nickname. (Which —now—fewer and fewer people knew.) *Strong as an ox.* This heroic epithet derived from a con he had perfected. He grabbed a chair or a small table at the foot of one leg and took bets as to whether he could lift it with one hand and hold it extended. That was the one he never lost. But now he was still known as Oxie only on Gimlet. The people he had any use for knew him as Ted Pape, which name was as close as he cared to come to Theodorik Paparikis, the name his parents gave him. . . .

He slapped his thighs and then rubbed his belly, kneading the skin between his knuckles. Huh-oh, better watch out. Beginning to buy himself a bit of a paunch. These days he couldn't get the exercise he ought to. He spent a lot of time at his A.C. but he used it up making contacts and running errands for himself. Never got a chance to work out . . . Well, he was going to have to be careful, have to take the time.

"Don't worry, baby. Everything's still there."

The woman's voice was thick with sleep, but there was no ill nature in her taunt. Instead, an amused complacency.

The sheets were bunched about her in such a way that Oxie

saw her face as a pink triangular patch stuck onto a blue-eyed rhomboid. (Was *this* what he'd paid for?) He answered with his customary softness. "Good morning, sweetheart. I was trying to keep quiet so I wouldn't wake you up. But I'm pretty clumsy. I wondered if I was waking you."

—A flat lie. He was trying to wake her; he didn't want the maid to come in and find her in the bed. For the maid he tried to keep up a front virginally respectable, and though he knew it was foolish to think he was successful at it the itch was still in him and he persisted week after week, months on end.

"I wondered if I *were* waking you," she said. "If: were."

"Sorry," he muttered.

Poor Oxie. No relief. Never a moment of truce he found.

Unhurriedly he began to dress. He got out his favorite comfortable shoes with the heavy antique buckles. Now how did it all fit together? Too jaunty maybe. Flippant? Ah what the hell. It was Saturday morning. Rubbed into the grain of his being, the Gimlet Street habit of thinking of Saturday as the big day, the day with the high sweet action. Saturday mornings he felt mildly exhilarated still, but he didn't quite know why.

"Hungry?" he said.

"I'm not sure yet. What do you have in mind?"

"I was thinking how I might get us a little breakfast. Toast and marmalade. Bacon and eggs. How's that sound?"

She threw back the sheets and scrambled for her slip. "No chance," she said. "I'll make it. You're not the type to be waiting on a woman. Didn't anybody ever tell you that?"

"I don't remember that it ever came up."

"You're just a liar." She came to him with her arms wide, nuzzled him on the cheek, put her tongue behind his ear. "Ha. You smell good. You smell rich."

He smiled shinily but abstractedly and slapped her lightly on the ass before she went into the bathroom and began running the water. Then he went out to the front door and got the newspaper and sat on the sofa to read. He lit another cigar and moved a bottle of Chivas Regal to the far side of the coffee table to make room for his ashtray.

By ten-thirty he was in the Brass Rail, one of the two new pool halls in town. He liked it here. Not much noise, cool beautiful fluorescent lights over the eight tables, a thick wine-colored carpet. Oxie had learned his game in joints like the Queen's Own and the Diamond, with lumpy tables, cues out of true, and fights breaking out every few minutes, or so it seemed. All that wasn't so bad; mostly he remembered feeling grateful whenever he was able to work up a game in those days. They hadn't been good days.

(Had they been happy days?)

(What is that supposed to mean? What's happiness got to do with it?)

Best thing in the Brass Rail was the thick carpet. Saved all that wear and tear on the feet. It seemed to Oxie that no matter how far ahead you got, you still spent your life standing. One of the wearying aspects of the business life.

He was engaged in a perfunctory game of rotation with Freene Sluder. Freene was a dope by anybody's standards. If Oxie felt free to choose his own company . . . But Freene had money, oh yes, and somehow he still managed to keep his seat on the city council, but Oxie knew for a fact that of the two cases his daddy's law firm had allowed him to handle this year Freene had won neither. Most of his dump (No, not dump. Money. Money is the word you use. Goddammit) came from his quarter interest in a prosperous roadhouse called The Cat and Spoon, a bootleg joint. Not white bootleg, though: bonded. At eleven at night or at one or three in the morning you could buy a fifth of Early Times at The Cat and Spoon if you didn't mind paying twelve dollars. . . .

There was the point where Freene's lack of brains betrayed him most thoroughly. He always wanted to hire the hardasses for drivers, hysterical violent guys who as often as not had picked up a little time here and there. Pickett was driving hooch for him now, Frankie Pickett. Oxie remembered when Frankie had pulled two of five down at Craggy for attempted child rape. When you hired hardasses you were begging for trouble. Just wait till Frankie got it in his head one of these first nights to strongarm The Cat and Spoon for a quick wad and then light out for Arkansas. That would be your profit for a solid week, at least. . . . Or he'd do something even dumber, you could trust Frankie. Maybe he'd show up drunk and stomp one of the customers. That would put Freene so far up the creek he couldn't see daylight. The cops would have to squeeze down on the joint; and Freene's old man would have to spend a pile bailing their names out of the newspapers. . . .

And all this trouble brought on because Freene thought if the hardasses looked mean and talked mean they had experience and you could trust them. Well, they had experience all right, but you couldn't trust them any more than you could trust wild dogs. Oxie could tell Freene, Oxie knew exactly what he was getting into. But he couldn't say anything without giving away his own history. He couldn't do that.

He had a hard time keeping even a minimum of interest in the pool game. Freene was deadly inept and Oxie had to take pains not to give it away that he was lagging his score just enough for the chattering bald man to be able to nose him out at the last moment. It almost didn't seem worth the trouble—till Oxie thought about the law practice. One of these days, when Freene's old man kicked off or retired from practice, Freene could throw Oxie a fair-sized chunk of business.

"Ted, what's the true scoop on the fight next week?"

Oxie smiled dimly. "Cassius has got it tied up in a sack, Freene. I don't have official odds yet, but I'm pretty sure they'll settle about eight to five in favor of Clay."

"You sure about that?"

"I won't know the Vegas odds till Tuesday, but I won't be far wrong."

"How about letting me know when you hear? You know, I been

106

thinking I might put something down against that loudmouth sombitch. One of these days somebody's got to take him."

"Maybe. One of these days. But it won't be next week. Before anybody puts him down, you and me will have long gray beards, Freene."

(No. Incorrect: you and I. Goddammit.)

(But Oxie wasn't sure Freene was up on his grammar any more. Huh. Been to college, too.)

"You sure about that now? I been thinking it was past time he got his."

"Well, if that's what you want. But don't go around saying I suckered you into that bet. Pick Clay and pick up your money. If you can find anybody to bet with."

Freene bent to level his eye with the table, inspecting the lie of a perfectly obvious shot. Oxie was certain Freene hadn't listened to a word he'd said; he was going right ahead and drop a hundred or so on the fight. And then afterward he would have to be careful what he said around him so that the dumb bastard wouldn't think he was rubbing it in. That was just one more thing to remember, work piled on top of work.

At last he got a bit of momentum and Oxie was able to lose the game with a semblance of grace. Now Freene became jolly and expansive; he stood Oxie a cup of coffee in the barroom and regaled him with a long involved account of a fishing trip he had gone on last month. Oxie kept a careful face and now and then asked a bland question. Finally it ended with Freene slapping him on the shoulder and inviting him to come out to the Sluder cabin on the lake one of these first weekends. (That was how he said it: "You got to come out the Sluder cabin one of these first days." God, what an asshole.) Out on the lake it was quiet and peaceful; they could loaf around and fish a little and do just whatever they pleased. . . . Carefully Oxie laughed off the invitation.

Fishing, for God's sake. Who had that kind of time to waste?

Oxie had never held a fishing rod in his hands. He had never seen anybody use one.

Then Freene said he had to run to the post office, he'd better get going. His daddy had sent him out to mail some deeds before he ran into Oxie.

"Well, take it easy," Oxie said. "Tell your daddy I said hello."

"Sure thing, I'll do that. Take it easy."

Through the bar window Oxie watched him go up the street toward the square, a tall bald-headed helter-skelter man who, even walking, seemed purposeless. When he was out of sight Oxie handed the bartender a small packet of tipsheets for the baseball games. They exchanged a few words, pleasant enough, but all business, and then Oxie left, whistling softly because he was happy, remembering at the last moment not to stuff his hands into his pockets.

The Brass Rail was a half block off the main square. Oxie went into the square, made a couple of stops at joints and came to the west corner. On his left was the equestrian statue of Zebulon Johns, Patriot and Philanthropist, looming green and solid in the bright midday light. Oxie was still preoccupied with Freene Sluder (that guy left a bad taste in your mouth) and he thought that right there stood the horse Freene would pick for the Belmont. If he was even that lucky. And then he thought that since he was here on the corner of Gimlet anyway he might as well check out Clemmie and Agnes. He turned right and started downhill.

Here he was, the old territory. He knew every inch of it, every wall, corner and door. He could point to every stain-shaped asphalt repairing of the pavement and tell you whether it was here when he'd been on Gimlet or had been put down later. He knew the graffiti painted on the bricks and the weeds that sprang up in the gravel-strewn alleys. And he knew the faces; especially he knew the faces. He knew everything.

He'd been, let's see, was it eleven years old when he took off from his folks. Not that they missed him, happy to see him go. Eight kids and no money: he harbored no bitterness. He lived in the stockroom of old man Kirschner's grocery store. A lousy

108

pallet on the floor and a lousy three bucks a week, and he'd had to sweep the place out morning and night, dust all the canned goods once a day and deliver whatever groceries they asked him to. That was no life even for a snotnose kid and it had lasted only six months. Then he'd moved into Bluebird Billiards and piled his blankets on the far table. Hook Matters was always threatening to have that table reslated and refelted but he never did, so it was all right for Oxie to take it. A hell of a lot better than the grocery store: the work wasn't so hard and he'd learned to shoot pool. It was then he'd begun to work up a little action of his own, just a little bit.

And then he was fourteen and he'd moved into the basement of the Park Hotel, into a tiny room that used to be a broom closet, next to the bottom of the elevator shaft. Made it hard to sleep, but in those days he didn't need much sleep anyway. Here he learned about women. Seemed that most of the Park girls took a shine to him. Ah Lord, he'd been a pretty child. They liked having him around to talk to, and he'd run and get cold drinks for them and every now and then one of them would get the blue devils and he'd sneak her in a bottle. In the Park Hotel he'd made his first contacts, got his first real start. That was because he liked girls, he didn't mind listening to them chatter. He used to wonder why some of these girls hadn't got ahead the way he had, they knew the johns so well and could take them by the short hairs anytime. . . . But he'd stopped wondering; the mauds just weren't like that. They just didn't use the information, passed it along to Oxie instead. The mauds were plenty smart, but that just wasn't their way.

He walked along, breathing lightly. Most of the faces he passed on the sidewalk were familiar to him. Guys nodded at Oxie or spoke to him and he smiled and saluted them but didn't speak. This was nice, really, to come back down here where people looked up to him, thought of him as a real success. Lord knows, the crowd he was running with these days didn't think of him like that. In fact he was curious how they did think of him.

109

A broad fat woman with a mottled face spoke to him as he paused for a moment under the edge of a shop awning to light his cigar.

"Hello, Oxie. Been a long time, ain't it?"

He had to peer at her closely: "Annie?"

"That's me. I've changed some, ain't I?"

He felt obscurely frightened and examined the glowing tip of his cigar. "You ought to lay off that damn hop, Annie. It's not doing you any good."

"You're right about that, Oxie. It gets me to where I can't eat. But then if I don't take it I get stomach cramps you wouldn't believe how awful. It ain't that easy." Her voice took on a tone of vague wonderment. "What I can't understand is how I got so fat."

"You ought to lay off."

"I know it. But it ain't as easy as saying it, Oxie."

"You want some money, Annie?"

"I didn't ask you for none."

"I can hear all right. You want some money?"

"Sure I do."

"Will five dollars do you any good?"

"Sure it will. I appreciate it, Oxie. . . . For old time sake, huh?"

"For old times, Annie."

Jesus Christ.

It couldn't have been so long ago—eleven, twelve years at most —she'd been the hottest thing going, one of the best-looking mauds on the sidewalk. The johns would turn in their tracks to follow her, a spell would come over them. Oxie had never had anything going with her, nothing like that. But he used to buy her a drink now and then just to have something pleasant to look at across the table. He'd listen to her carry on about various and sundry, and they'd got to be friendly. But look at her now. . . . Involuntarily he shuddered. He'd seen it enough times, but still . . . Hop was bad stuff.

(They say it made you feel all warm inside, right in the pit of your stomach.)

110

He went into the Ace. Nobody here but John the barkeep and that lush, Teacher, reading one of his idiot books. He gave Teach a brief nod and called into the other room where John was mopping up.

"John buddy, how's it going?"

"Going fine, Oxie. How's it with you?"

"Just fine, fine. Say, has Clemmie been in this morning?"

"Ain't seen her."

"If she happens to drop by tell her I'm looking for her, will you?"

"Sure thing."

He went out, turning his face gratefully to the sunlight. It felt good. He was always happier with summer coming on. Maybe because he'd been so cold as a kid . . .

He tried a couple of other joints but no one had seen her. Probably she was sleeping late; a busy Friday night could be hard on the girls. He decided to give up for a while, walked on down and pushed into the Mutt and Jeff lunch. An odd place, though long and narrow like so many of them. It was run by two true losers he had some fondness for. On one side was a counter with stools where you could buy hot dogs and Pepsis and not another blessed thing, unless you wanted to take a chance on a ten-year-old package of peanuts. Against the other wall were lined three old church pews set up on a plywood platform. He climbed up and sat in the corner of a pew and Bobby came zooming down the aisle, bowling the johns out of the way with his wheelchair.

"Whoo-ee, gawd-damn. Get out of my way, younguns, and let me get a peep at them faggot-looking shoes Oxie's got on. Whoo, whoo." Like a steam engine.

Bobby had an extremely thick torso and powerful arms, but both his legs had been amputated. He talked incessantly in a low-pitched gritty voice. He rolled the chair to Oxie and halted it suddenly; if it had been a car the tires would have screeched.

"Bobby, how's it going?"

"Going straight down, going to hell. Done gone to hell, couldn't drag it back with a log chain. Ain't been a sign of life around here since old granny got her tits caught in the washing machine."

"Does seem quiet these days."

"That ain't the word. Makes the First Baptist graveyard look like a sailors' gangbang."

"What'll you take for a shine?"

"Shine these? Hadn't you ought to kill em first?"

"Listen to you. These are the going shoes, Bobby. What you got against these shoes?"

"They all right. I can see how they might be useful. Long as you got them on ain't nobody going to law you for paternity."

"Man comes in here to give you some honest business and all he gets is insults. You must be awful rich, to treat your customers that way. You going to give me a shine or not? I can always take my trade to The Nigger."

"Might be as how he's the only one can do it right. I'm going to have to mix up a special polish for these here queerass things. You want me to scrub up them gold-plate buckles?"

"I don't care," Oxie said. "Just do it right."

Bobby reached into the stained canvas bags that hung on both sides of his wheelchair and brought out handful after handful of shoe polish tins. He rejected all the cans but two. These he opened and, after mixing the waxes on a new clean rag, began working the stuff into the leather. He started telling Oxie all about Enos, his eighteen-year-old boy. Enos had got into racing stock cars. He'd fixed up an old '56 Ford with a hell of a good '62 Mercury motor, and every Friday night and Saturday night and then all day every Sunday he was out somewhere tearing up the cow pastures. "I told him he wouldn't never get no pickup out of that rig. I told him, I says, That old washing machine wouldn't pull a greasy string out of a cat's ass. But he went to work on it, I never seen the beat of elbow grease, and I swear it does okay now. Runs sweet, what I tell you. I wouldn't never have thought. He's picked him up a little bit of prize money here and there, but naturally he pours it right back into that car. You better put some of

112

that away, I told him. One of these days some science feller will come up with something different than shoes for people to wear and I won't have nothing to give you. Then what'll you do for cash money? But it don't matter what I tell him. Water off a duck's back."

Bobby had finished the leather. He wheeled back a foot or so and stared musingly at Oxie's feet. "Tell you what, Oxie, I don't think I ought to mess with them buckles. Shine em up and they'll lose that goldy-looking color. I think they're supposed to keep a kind of old-timey look."

"You're the doctor, Bobby. How much do I owe you?"

"Every bit of thirty-five cents."

"Thirty-five? Wasn't so long ago it was an even quarter."

"Tell you though, Oxie, they went up on the price of T-bone steaks. You know I won't eat nothing else."

Oxie gave him a dollar. "Here you go. Save some of it for Santy Claus."

"Now that's what I call a sporting man," Bobby said.

Oxie retraced his steps. It was getting late, almost noon. If he didn't catch up with Clemmie pretty soon he would have to let it go until another day. That would be awkward, mean another trip maybe. But he had to be in the jail at the drunk tank at lunchtime. If he got there at mealtimes they would be taking the sandwiches in to the birds and he could go in with them. Any off-hour, and they had to make an extra trip up the stairs and unlock just for him. Cops were like anybody else; they didn't like to do any more than they could help. Oxie had to stay on their good side, and they remembered little things like that. It was that bit of thoughtfulness kept you in the gravy.

But he was in luck. When he got back to the Ace Clemmie was sitting at the bar talking to Teacher.

He hesitated. Why was it that it always took him a moment or two actually to recognize Clemmie? Between this time and the last he honestly couldn't remember what she looked like. But she didn't look bad, not really. A tiny bit of a woman, about five-two;

113

thin as a rifle barrel. Hatchet-faced. God help us, what hair. You wouldn't believe hair like that would grow on a human person; it was more like the old horse's tail. No, it was more like long broomstraw, beaten and battered and frazzled. It wasn't hard to see how she would pick up her fair share of business all right, something about her that would make the johns turn and look if nothing else. For Oxie, of course, she held no attraction, no more than a razor or table or wallet he owned. Mechanism still in running order. Something doing what it was supposed to do with a minimum of attention.

She shrieked when she saw him. "Why howdy there, stranger," she cried. "I aint seen you it seems like years. Where in the world you ever been to, Arkansas?"

"Clemmie," he said, remembering to be gentle, to go easy. He led her to a corner where they could talk without Teacher listening in. Lushes had loose mouths. Dutifully Oxie pulled her chair out for her, carefully avoiding having to touch her. Touching Clemmie made him feel soiled and—well, greasy. He didn't know why. . . . He sat and ordered two cups of coffee.

"How's the world treating you these days?" he said.

"What?" She was staring at him.

Slow down, Oxie, he thought. He kept forgetting how dogass dumb she was.

"I just asked how everything was going, Clemmie. Are you keeping yourself alive?"

She showed her small sharp teeth in an overeager smile. "I been doing fine," she said. "Of course now, I missed *you*. Seems like it's been an awful long time."

He sighed. "Always the same old thing, sweetheart. Business and more business. Just never get the chance no more to sit down and chat with my old friends. A real shame."

It went on like that. Oxie gentled her along, kept her talking, and talking himself only when it was absolutely necessary. Both of them knew exactly why he was there—Oxie had come to collect his money, simple as that. But when you were dealing with

114

women you didn't come out in the open with much. Nothing straight on the line. First you had to talk about everything under the sun and at the bottom of the ocean. Or, more accurately, you had to listen. That was the trick with women, you had to know how to listen. When he was a young squirt it had been countless times he'd screwed the deal with some maud just because he'd let himself get impatient. Well, a man learns some things, just give him time enough.

"Well now. You say things have been going pretty good. No complaints?"

"I guess not. Everything's just fine."

So Oxie settled himself. This familiar prelude meant that she had grievances against everybody on the street.

"But Squelch . . . You know Squelch, the barhop down at the Big Bunny. Somebody ought to take him down a notch or two. Bet you I know somebody one of these days who'll do it too. Well, anyway. The other night I was in there with Harold. You know, Harold. Who's got that real light hair, real good-looking, and those real deep blue eyes? I was in the Bunny there with him, and of course Harold had been drinking some, but not all that much and I know because I was with him just about the whole time. He wasn't falling down or sick or nothing like that. Anyway, Squelch said for me to get him sobered up some or he was going to kick both of us out. And keep us out. Brother, you ought to heard what I said to him. . . ."

She talked her way from the Big Bunny, to Maxie's, to the Champagne Club. Just making the rounds. Oxie thought for a moment that she was going to cover every joint in the territory and he sneaked a glance at the wall clock. He still had time to get to jail before lunch, but it was going to be too late to catch up with Agnes. . . . Clemmie went on. She told him of course that she'd been sick and had to stay off the street some days. He knew that story well enough.The mauds always had that story ready to forestall any gripes you might have about the amount of money they handed over. And she'd got into a fight or two. Oxie knew

115

that too. Clemmie's worst fault. One of these first nights some-body was going to break that skinny little neck. . . . And Arkie had been annoying her, talking crazy.

Arkie.

Arkie?

"Wait a minute," he said. "Who is this Arkie person?"

A pretense of surprise. "Why. I thought you knowed him. He says you do. Of course, he'll say just about anything. All the way he knows to talk is pure crazy."

"I'm not quite sure. Who is he exactly?"

"You must of seen him around. He's always around, getting in people's way. . . . He ain't nobody really. Kind of a midgety little guy, always in these cafes running two-bit con jobs on sol-diers and people. He ain't nobody. Ain't a soul on the street that pays him no never-mind."

Something in Clemmie's voice hooked at Oxie's mind. She was talking faster than usual, she was trying to gloss over some-thing. It might be like she said, that this was just a zero character not worth thinking about, but Oxie listened carefully to her de-scription. An undertow of excitement in her breathing. Whatever this kid had said it meant something to Clemmie.

". . . Just always talking crazy. He don't count for nothing."

He thought he remembered. "Blond-haired kid? Wears a blue rayon blazer with white stripes on the sleeves?"

She widened her eyes. "Yeah. That's him, that's Arkie. Why? Is he a buddy of yours?"

"Well, not hardly." (More like a cousin, maybe, or a young half brother.) Oxie laughed softly. He'd seen the kid around, juicing the johns and the mules and the gunghoes, working out on anybody that came within reach. The picture of him stayed in Oxie's head because when he saw him he couldn't help remem-bering the way he himself had come along. Most of the same old cons still seemed to work. Over the years the Gimlet Street cli-entele wasn't getting any smarter. So that was his name, then: Arkie. Oxie thought of him as looking fiercely hungry. "I've seen

116

him around," he said. "You know, I had him pegged as a guy who'd probably be needing me one of these first days. But it occurred to me that when he did I wouldn't be able to help him at all."

And that was true enough. So many times Oxie had spotted them, starting the same way he'd started, but ending up in the state's watch pocket.

Clemmie laughed, stridently and too loudly. She seemed relieved.

"Just what has this Arkie person been saying, anyhow?"

He saw that she hesitated nervously. Man, that runty little kid had dropped something that got to her.

She began speaking even more quickly, trying to get it all out in a lump. "It was all pure crazy. He said that you was awful busy these days. He said that you had lots of different business deals, all your other business deals didn't leave you hardly no time whatever and that anyhow you was getting fed up. Fed up with me, is what he meant. He made me the proposition, he wanted me to come in on the business with him." She halted suddenly and breathed deeply. Her coffee spoon trembled on the edge of the table. "What he said, you was getting set to cut loose of me and Agnes. You was too busy and he could take a lot better care."

Well, Jesus.

In fact, the kid was sharp. Getting rid of Clemmie and Agnes was an attractive notion, and Oxie had been thinking about it off and on for a while now. One of these days—he could foresee it— he was going to have to cut his connections with them. If he could only get headed right in the direction he meant to go, if he could get it set up clean, he'd have to bid them a sweet goodbye. Because if you got legitimate you had to keep legitimate, you didn't want anybody digging up tie-ins with prostitution or gambling or anything else that would hinder your access to political money. If you were the pieraker yourself, if you could stand election or get yourself appointed, that was different. A little scandal didn't hurt so much. But if you were in Oxie's shoes, in

117

the position of selling your services to politicians, you had to be specially careful. The politicians would drop you flat, cut you off quick. They wouldn't speak to you. They'd stand on the courthouse steps and swear on a Bible that they'd never laid eyes on you.

But just now he wasn't ready to let the girls go. They still brought in money, or at least Clemmie did. Maybe not so much, but it helped. Oxie still hadn't quite turned the corner; it wasn't yet terribly important whether or not he was entirely legitimate, so why let the money go to waste? The time to get free of them was not when you could afford to, but when you couldn't afford *not* to. . . . He was confident that he would recognize the moment.

He let himself laugh. "That kid's got some wild imagination. He ought to go on the television."

"He's just a dumb runt."

She was giggling again, and now her relief was open, obvious. She was happy once more; he'd said the right things, punched the buttons in correct sequence. He let her run on a few minutes longer, trilling her recent autobiography like a caged canary, but the hour was growing late. When her monologue came round another full circle—she began again on her imagined illness—he cut her short. "Now I've told you. Don't worry your pretty head about the money. I know how things go sometimes. I want you to know I've got a world of confidence in you." He kept adding sugary nothings—it was like stuffing a pillowcase with cotton candy—and he speculated idly about how much she was knocking down on him. He didn't really care one way or another. Let her get what she could. For damn sure, one of these days she was going to need it. He readied himself to leave, tacking on the old line about a lunch date with her. Clemmie liked that one, always reacted as if he'd never mentioned anything like it before.

Finally he rose and held her chair as she too got up. "See you at two then," he said.

"Back here?"

Let's see, she had been complaining about the barkeep at the

Big Bunny. He might as well talk to Squelch and tell him to let up a little on the maud. Squelch owed him a favor, and since it didn't cost anything to make Clemmie more satisfied . . . "No, let's get together down at the Big Bunny. That would be closer for me. Maybe I can see Agnes too."

As he was going out the studious form of Teacher caught his eye and he stopped, lazily impulsive. He took the book from Teacher's hands and flipped over the cover.

Jesus God on a flagpole: outer space. Going to the moon. Movie monsters.

"How come you want to read this kind of trash? Doesn't do you any good, does it? I'd think it was a complete waste."

"It's just something to pass the time," Teacher said. He had a squeaky little voice. "I don't take it serious."

"Well, I'll tell you a book," Oxie said. "One you can really get some good out of. It's called *How to Win Friends and Influence People.* I've read it twice from cover to cover."

Oxie left. He thought both Clemmie and Teacher ought to feel grateful toward him.

He had to cross the square again, beginning this time at the southeast corner, going past the Stanza Theater, the library, the Gospel Light Book Shop, the fire station. He strode along easily, swinging his arms slightly. He was still happy in the new warm weather, and when he got to the police station he almost bounded up the steps. (But of course did not. It would have been a serious breach of decorum.) Going down the battered familiar corridor he whistled softly through his teeth.

"Morning, sergeant."

"Hello, Ted. Go on up if you want to. It's right now lunchtime."

"All right. Thanks."

He mounted the stairs and rapped on the door and was admitted. The second door was standing open, so he went directly into the cell block.

It seemed an ordinary enough Friday night's crop. There were about fifteen men. Their clothes were damp and a couple of them were shivering. That meant they had been a little rambunctious last night and had got hosed down for their horniness. (Dumb bastards; some guys never learned.) They didn't look so fired up this morning. Wet clothes and a hangover don't allow you much fighting room. The greasy egg sandwiches had already been doled out to them, and they held them carefully in one hand while with the other they stretched through the bars the flimsy paper cups. All lined up, pressed against the bars one after another. Borden, a thin cop who never stood close enough to his razor, passed down the line pouring lukewarm coffee from a scratched steel bottle with a tiny spout.

The hefty cop, Lubrani, spoke to Oxie. He stood in the outside aisle cuddling his night stick in his arm like a football. "Hi, Ted. You here to let all the birds out?"

"Morning, Nello. I'm here simply to help those who need help."

He went to the bars, carefully avoiding the patches of water on the floor, and taking care also not to breathe too deeply. Today it didn't smell as bad as usual—probably because of the hosing— but it was an odor that annoyed Oxie every time. He looked over his prospects, at first sight not very promising. He spotted Jeddie Mangum, who'd probably been unzipping his fly for some kid in a movie house. Nothing for Oxie there, Jeddie's sister would beg him off again. (Jail was no good for that guy anyway. Why didn't they put him somewhere that might help?) And there was the usual clutch of drunks: Burke Palmer, Marvin Garrett, Craig Walker, Arthur Bailey. All drunks, and nothing there for Oxie. They wouldn't pay him bail money because Monday they'd be free anyway after a seventeen-dollar fine. But they'd picked up Frankie Pickett, and Oxie went quickly to talk to him.

"Frankie," Oxie said. "Man, what in the world you doing here? Somebody make a mistake?"

He wouldn't keep his eyes fixed on Oxie; looked at everything else, the floor, the walls, the bars, his hands. "Bet your ass it's a mistake. They's somebody going to be awful sorry about this."

"What happened?"

120

"It wasn't none of my goddam fault. This old girl I know, see, and she invited me over to drink a beer or two. Well, another dumb maud in there and . . ."

"Well, that's all right," Oxie said. "Don't bother about that part." He could have guessed it already. Crazy goddam hardass, liked to beat up on women. One of Freene Sluder's loveliest jewels, Frankie was. "Have they set bail yet?"

"Not yet. Least, I don't reckon they have." He wouldn't keep his eyes still.

"Freene know they've picked you up?"

"No by God he don't," Frankie said, "and when he finds out there's by God some of these blueball sons of bitches going to hear about it. They don't know who they've been messing with. They going to be awful sorry."

"Well now, you keep calm and don't worry. Won't be any trouble. I'll have you out before you know it." Usually when Oxie tendered this ritual but genuine assurance he reached through the bars to shake hands with the bird. Not this time. He was damned if he was going to shake hands with Frankie Pickett.

"Look, you just tell Freene where I am. He'll let these bastards know where to get off."

"Right," Oxie said. "I'll sure tell him."

He went on down the aisle, glad to be leaving Frankie. More of the familiar crew, no use to Oxie. And there was a high school student, or anyway a kid dressed like a high school student. (Like a bum, in Oxie's eyes.) But not a bad-appearing kid: clear gray eyes, clean dark hair, no really bad complexion problem. Oxie glanced at his hands, saw that his fingernails were well kept. That pegged him as coming from a good family, dead certain. And there was something else about him. . . . What? . . . Something Oxie couldn't remember. He stepped to the bars and beckoned. "Hey son, come here a minute."

The kid rose obediently from the bench where he had been eating—reluctantly, it seemed—and came to stand before Oxie, still holding his coffee and his sandwich.

"What's your name, son?"

121

He smiled. Kind of a sad smile. "I'm sorry, sir. I can't say. I haven't been telling that to anyone."

"Yeah?" Even for a kid he must not be too smart.

"Yes sir."

"Family trouble?"

He paused. "I guess so. In a way."

"Well now. You couldn't have been up to anything really bad."

"I don't know, sir. It was bad enough to get me in here."

"It would probably make it a whole lot easier if you let people know who you are."

He shook his head. "I'd rather not do that."

"Wait now. Look, I'm not a policeman, I'm a bondsman. You know what that is?"

"No sir."

"I'm somebody who helps people when they're in trouble, I help them get out of jail. . . . Wait a minute." He felt about in his pockets, then drew out a business card. Oxie was proud of his card. He'd designed it himself; that is, the printer had been able to reproduce a couple of his suggestions—not as many as Oxie had hoped. He always carried cards with him, and when he'd first got them printed up he'd given them out to almost everyone he knew. It ran into money, sure, but it was worth it for the impression of legitimacy they gave. The card showed a bulbous little cartoon character in a business suit. On his shoulders were tiny angel wings and a wind-streaked cloud was sketched into the background. Are you IN and you want OUT? Be as FREE as a BIRD! And in the right-hand corner, his name with his home phone number and the number of Brass Rail Billiards.

(Damn good advertising. Caught the eye. Smarter than those insurance agent cards you saw all the time.)

The boy read the card, smiling again even more faintly.

"Why don't you tell me your name so I can let your daddy know where you are? I'll bet you he's worried sick."

He shook his head.

"I promise I won't tell the officers. Word of honor."

122

"No sir."

"Well, you know what you're doing. Or do you?"

"No sir. But I'd rather not say right now."

Oxie started to walk away, but then stopped and turned to the boy once more. He felt regretful without knowing exactly why. Something wiggled at the bottom of his mind. What was he over-looking? The kid was from a good family, no mistaking that. Maybe even from a wealthy family. That was plenty of opportunity. If he could find out who the boy was and get word to his father there would more than likely be something in it for Oxie. More than just cash money. It might be he would be establishing a solid connection, something that could help him out uptown. It might lead to anything, a real move, the kind you kept hoping for. . . . He gave the boy a fresh look. He was muttering, "There's something about you that reminds me of—" he fingered his moustache "—reminds me of a schoolteacher." He wasn't really talking to the kid; talking more to himself. And he almost didn't say "schoolteacher" but "Teacher." Teacher, that lush, already early in the morning planted on his ass in the Ace, drinking and reading. Crazy damn thought: Teach was a dumb drunk, worn out, and here was this fresh clean-cut kid, almost baby-faced.

He'd startled the boy. He looked apprehensive. Began an in-voluntary blurted sentence: "My father is a tea—"

"What, son?" Very gently.

"Nothing. Nothing, sir."

Oxie moved on, noting perfunctorily that there were no other birds in the cage who'd offer him any business. Something gnawed at a corner of his mind.

The kid's father was a schoolteacher. Well, that was okay. Oxie had had some random dealings with schoolteachers. Probably not much money involved—though you couldn't be sure about that, either—but maybe some connections. Teachers had to have connections. They worked for the state, didn't they?

But that wasn't quite what was nagging at him.

He went back out into the anteroom of the cell block. Joshed

123

with the cops; made his manners. Downstairs he thanked the desk sergeant almost solemnly; chatted; gave him a cigar, departing.

Corny goddam business, handing out cigars like a pieraker on the make. But what else could you offer that wasn't either too cheap or too expensive?

(And at Christmas it was those goddam corny fruitcakes.)

(Maybe this year Scotch might go better?)

As he was walking through the parking lot it came to him why the boy had reminded him of Teacher. Bloomed in his memory like a sudden red and yellow flower. It was that crazy book Teach had been reading.

Outer space, weird planets.

Monsters from Mars.

The boy was in with that kind of stuff, he'd seen his face in the newspapers. He wrote down that kind of trash, or collected it, or something. Ate it for breakfast maybe. Anyhow, there had been a long write-up and pictures. If Oxie found the right paper he'd find the kid's name and address and parents, all he wanted to know. . . . He thought. To give a lot of space to that sort of junk—it would just about have to be a Sunday paper. And it couldn't have been too long ago or he wouldn't have remembered it—definitely not Oxie's kind of thing. Four or five weeks ago, it must have been. He thought.

If you wanted old newspapers you could go to the library. Library kept big files of them, and it was only half a block away. But Jesus Christ. Oxie had never been in a library. How would you go about finding anything? How were you supposed to act inside of a library? He didn't even know if he was dressed right. Jesus.

But there it was: they had what he needed to know.

He went, a bit uneasily now, straight along the south side of the square and stopped in front of the Zebulon Johns Memorial Library. Big mothering place. There was a revolving door, like the S&W cafeteria door, and this surprised him. When he pushed through he found himself in a small musty-smelling lobby lined

124

with wooden filing cabinets with hundreds of small drawers. In the center of the lobby was a circular counter-desk inside which two women were messing around with piles of white cards.

He went tentatively to the desk and one of the women accosted him. A tall brunette with a thin mouth and a square jaw, nose like a fingernail file. Just the kind of maud that made his skin crawl.

He felt helpless and belligerent at once.

"Yes sir," she said. "Can I help you?" Sound of her voice didn't seem to offer much aid. Like one of those tough nurses. *Now this won't hurt a bit;* while behind her back she's holding a needle the size of a baseball bat and can't wait to jam it into your suffering ass.

"Uh. Do you, do . . ." Too fucking silly. "Where do you keep the newspapers?"

She gestured with a bloodless thin wrist. "The periodical room is in there." She went back to piddling with her cards; Oxie knew he'd vanished from her mind.

He put his hands in his pockets but took them out again immediately. The wide doorway she'd pointed out actually opened into two rooms. The one on the right he supposed was the library proper. Shelves of books. Shelf after shelf. Look at them. Jesus. Must be tons and tons of books in there. Why would you need so many? No use in it. Oxie's belligerence was bordering on real anger.

In the room on the left people sat at four long oak tables leafing through magazines. Stuffed plastic armchairs scattered about, and in one of them an old guy sat reading a newspaper. It would be his luck that this skinny old bastard would have the exact newspaper Oxie wanted, and then how would he get it? But when he drew closer he saw that the headlines weren't in English. He couldn't read them. This guy was some dumb spick, he bet. Not even an American.

He spotted other newspapers hanging spindled on the racks like sides of beef in a slaughterhouse and he took them down

125

awkwardly and looked through them. But they were all too recent, yesterday's or from the day before. Even the ones from England weren't more than a week old. He felt eyes upon him and turned. The old geezer with the spick newspaper was staring at him through his wire-rimmed glasses. He had a big Adam's apple and thin patches of gray hair. Suddenly Oxie felt like lifting him up and squeezing him in his hands. He would crackle and break like dry straw. Oxie could shred him and wad him and except for the snapping of his dry bones he wouldn't make a sound.

He glanced about him, grimly certain. He was never going to find out anything in here.

When he went back into the lobby the women didn't even glance at him and he shoved determinedly through the door. He stood on the sidewalk, furious. Goddam sons of bitches. Got no juice in them, they were bloodless as shoelaces. Shameful, that a man had to put up with all that just to get his hands on an old newspaper.

He stood thinking what he might do, and when the answer occurred to him he felt better instantly, laughed softly. No, man, those sickly creeps wouldn't have you by the shorts. He crossed the square and got his big blue Buick out of the Brass Rail parking lot. He drove fourteen blocks down Rance Avenue to McCabe's Body and Fender Repair. He drove slowly, cruising along easily; thrust an oblong of Dentyne into his mouth.

This was so much easier. His territory, they knew him here. (Everybody knows Oxie.) He found Jack Harloe and shook hands, careful not to brush against the tall man's paint-spattered coveralls.

"Good God, Oxie, where you been? Been a month of Sundays."

"Hello, Jack. Nowhere special. Round and about."

"You come to see us for a A-1 paint job on that beat-up old Buick?"

"What're you talking, beat-up? Don't have seven thousand on her yet."

126

"Well then. You just want to get rid of that ugly color."

Oxie laughed. "Not today, babe."

"Don't think somebody'll shoot you, driving that queer-appearin blue around here?"

"Better not. I'm liable to shoot back."

"Ha. Yeah. That's the way. . . . What can I do for you, then?"

"Well, if you don't mind, I'd kind of like to look through your old newspapers."

"Newspapers? When did you learn how to read? I didn't hear about it."

"I didn't learn so well, actually. Thought I might practice up."

"Christ, help yourself. There's sure enough of them." He pointed a battered and polychrome hand at four great stacks of papers leaning tipsy in one corner of the shop.

"Okay, man. Thank you. Buy you a drink sometime."

"Hey, babe, watch yourself now. I might take you up on that."

They kept the newspapers here, hundreds of them, to mask windows and whatever other areas of the cars they didn't want sprayed with paint. Cut the papers to fit and attached them with long strips of tape. The papers here were in no kind of order and they were grimy with metallic particles of paint that settled on them from the sanding of the car bodies. He would get his hands filthy and probably his clothes, and that was too bad.

But it wasn't as bad as that mothering library. Nothing was.

He began searching, and he was lucky. (The luck was holding sharp today.) In less than half an hour he'd found the paper he needed. He read the story carefully.

YOUNG SKYLARKS LOOK TO FUTURE.

There you go.

The kid's name was Linn Harper. He was the son of Andrew T. and Katherine Harper, residing at 1453 Wedgewood Drive. Andrew T. Harper was an assistant professor of history here at William Watson College.

See, he'd been right. You got to trust your instincts.

But maybe he'd been wrong about how much money they had.

Wedgewood Drive was located in Otter Lake, one of the most expensive of the residential suburbs.

Oxie cut out the story with his small silver penknife, folded it and put it into his wallet. He went to say good-bye to Jack Harloe.

"Find what you were looking for, Oxie?"

"Found what I needed," he said. Feeling expansive. "Thanks a lot, Jack. I appreciate it."

"Well hell, I didn't do nothing. Them papers just set there."

"Thanks anyhow. I'm serious about that drink."

"Watch it now."

"You take it easy."

"Any way I can get it."

"There you go," Oxie said.

Exhilarated, he drove back to the Brass Rail. He hummed a silly Dean Martin tune and tapped his fingernails on the steering wheel in time to it. He went into the bar and told Bill to send down a fifth of J&B to Jack Harloe at McCabe's body repair shop. "And send me in a couple of bourbons, Bill. I'm going to be in the back conference room for a while."

He almost laughed as Bill's face registered unbelieving surprise. Well, it *was* unusual. Oxie was no lush, a steady businessman. Wouldn't be twice in a year you'd see him drinking so early in the day.

Ha.

This was some special day, though. Man ought to celebrate luck. Unlucky not to.

He ducked into the bathroom, locked it and stripped off his shirt and undershirt. He washed the paint dust off his face and neck and arms and chest, and patted himself dry with a dozen rough paper towels. Put on his shirt and carefully retied the green suede tie. Inspected himself. Spat his gum-cud into the urinal.

He went into the small paneled "conference" room—actually a poker room—and sat at the round table covered with meditative

128

blue felt and put his feet up in one of the chairs. He leaned back and pressed together 'hard the fingertips of both hands. Bill brought the drinks in and set them down easy before him.

"There you go, drinking man."

"Thank you, Bill. I surely appreciate it."

"You seem awful happy right about now."

"I think maybe I am," Oxie said. "There's a fair chance I might be."

"Hope so."

In fact, he felt that he'd got something, but he didn't know exactly what it was. He took an Imperial Corona from his jacket pocket and lit it and crossed his ankles. He rubbed his moustache, fished at his crotch. He closed his eyes and opened his mouth, ran his tongue slowly across the sharp edges of his teeth. He sat like this for a while. When he remembered to puff at his cigar it had burned down a good half inch, holding a sleeve of pleasant gray ash. He went to a small table in a corner of the room and opened a drawer and took out a telephone directory. Leafed through it almost idly before underlining a number with his impeccable thumbnail.

Then he called.

"Hello. Who'm I talking to, please? . . . Mrs. Harper, my name is Ted Pape. I wonder if I might speak to your husband . . . Oh, I see . . . Yes mam, I understand . . . Well then, say I call back about three-thirty . . . Would that be all right? . . . Yes mam, it *is* pretty important . . . Yes mam, Pape. P-a-p-e . . . All right, thank you. Thank you very much."

He hung up.

It had gone as he had expected.

He sighed happily, and maybe a little nostalgically also. Oxie saw this moment as a turning point in his life. Anytime later he could look back and put his finger on it with all certainty and say, Well, that was where it all started. How often in his life would a man be able to say that? And it was true. He had it all figured out. The only unpleasantness remaining, the only piece of old business hanging on, was the matter of Clemmie and Agnes. That wouldn't take long. It was going to be troublesome, but it wouldn't take long.

He dialed another number—this one he didn't have to look up—and got hold of Freene Sluder and made an appointment to meet him at nine the next morning. He gave him the news about his employee, Frankie Pickett, making it as brief as possible. (But laying it out easily and carefully. Christ, you had to be careful with Freene.)

"Well, I'm damned." On the telephone the bald man's voice was screechy, irritatingly feminine. "I'll be goddamned."

"It's a bad piece of business," Oxie said.

"I'll nail his stupid ass to the goddam barn door," Freene said. "What did they haul him in for, you find out?"

"Cops that arrested him weren't on duty, but I think it might be trouble with the ladies. From what he said. I think he must have assaulted some woman."

"Dumbass son of a bitch. Not the first time, either. He's been in trouble like this before. I'm going to rake his ass over the slow coals, I'm telling you, Ted."

Oxie murmured on, calm and methodical. But he was nettled. Talking to Freene was like trying to talk to a fire engine siren going full blast. You had to wait until he ran down completely. "They'll probably set bail Monday. Tuesday at the latest. I told the man down at the station that I'd meet whatever the bond was as soon as they had it set. I'm sure there won't be any hitch about getting him out."

There was a long pause before Freene began again, his voice taking a new coloration now. ". . . Well, Ted, it's not that we don't appreciate it. We certainly do." (Oh, for Christ's bleeding sake. Dumb son of a bitch was starting to talk down to Oxie.) "And we sure don't mind throwing some business your way. Always glad to do that. Us buddies ought to stick together." (God. Buddies, already.) "But Ted, considering your interest rates and all, it would be cheaper for us if we went the bail ourselves. Actually, it would be a lot simpler."

Momentarily Oxie felt a kind of cheap pity for the man. . . . But Lord, how was he going to handle him now?

"Uh, well. Yeah, Freene, I see your point. But I think it might be wiser if you'd talk to your daddy about it first. You understand what I mean? Because if it is assault—and I'm pretty sure it is—then it's a fairly serious charge. That means it'll go in the newspaper and they'll probably also print the names of the people who have put up bail for Frankie. In your case they'll say that the bail was posted by Frankie's employers, and they'll put it in print—Freene Sluder and whatever other owners there are of The Cat and Spoon. You might better talk to your daddy. May be that he's not exactly craving for that kind of publicity right now. Seems to me it might not be the best thing in the world for the law office."

Freene was already too excited, his mouth was racing, his voice raised to its former screech. "Son of a bitch. I was clean forgetting that. Maybe it would be better for you to take care of it, Ted. And I wish you'd see what you can do to keep our names out of it."

"Long as I handle it there shouldn't be any trouble," Oxie said. "I'll keep it quiet. And don't be worrying about my rates. I'll give you a good price. Professional discount, Freene."

"We appreciate it, Ted. Certainly do. And don't you forget now we got a date to go fishing one of these days."

"Right," Oxie said. "Looking forward to it."

He made his voice sound friendly and casual before he hung up.

Well. That much was in hand, anyway, and glad to have it. (But look at the damage to the nerves.)

Now it was almost two o'clock and he remembered he'd made a date to meet Clemmie. Where was that? Oh yes, the Bunny. The Big Bunny. He remembered also that he hadn't yet eaten lunch, but he really wasn't hungry. Truth of the matter, he felt too happy to be hungry.

Her face showed bitter and livid and her acid green eyes

burned strangely. Oxie thought for a moment that she might try to attack him, shrieking and scratching and biting desperately, but she didn't. She slapped at the money on the table and the bills flurried up and settled, scattering on table and floor.

"Hell with the money. What about me? What do you expect I'm going to do?"

An odd thing: when you felt calm yourself and someone else was all wrought up it was a comical situation. Distantly comical: Oxie felt as if he were enclosed in a large, perfectly clear plastic box, sitting inside without worries and observing an exhibition the girl was giving for his benefit. He had to bear down hard to keep from laughing aloud. Huh-uh. No, man, that really would ruin it. And it wasn't that he was a stony-hearted guy; he could sympathize with old Clemmie. She had her point—felt that he was leaving her out in the cold cold weather. Or throwing her to the wolves. Or whatever. But that was because she couldn't see his side of it. Really, there was nothing else he could do. Here was the time when he couldn't afford *not* to free himself of Clemmie and Agnes. It was a simple business proposition.

To keep himself from laughing he lowered the register of his voice and spoke even more softly. Even to Oxie it didn't sound quite right—sounded ghostly; but he went on talking. "Oh, you'll make out fine, a girl with your looks."

"Shit."

She was making it awful hard not to laugh at her. She'd already begun picking up the money and piling it on the table. He knew her too well. Half an hour from now she'd be shaking hands with herself for conning Oxie out of it. He knew her kind too well. He chewed the inside corner of his lip.

She was trying to pull herself together and she wouldn't look him straight in the eye. Her face was red, her neck reddening. "Tell me this. Who's going to talk to the cops for me? They'll be at me every minute. Who's going to keep these goddam barhops in line? They'll gouge me for every penny I get hold of. Who's going to keep them in line? Tell me that."

132

Who? Who?

Like a goddam owl.

"It's not as bad as you're trying to make out," Oxie said. "There's a lot of people I might worry about but Clemmie's not one of them. You're too smart and good-looking."

He had set conscientiously about the job of trying to gentle her down, he would like to bring her around to where she could listen to sense. But it was a difficult proposition and his ebullience about his new prospects hampered him. His patience—Freene Sluder had already badly ravaged it—was beginning to give out. He was tired now of the whole business and he was glad to be coming to the end of it.

"What I can't figure out is why. I never done you bad, I never knocked down on you. I can't figure out why, is all."

His patience broke. This simple customary hypocrisy had stretched it too far. He was too close to the end of it, too close to the goals he'd always wanted to accomplish, and he couldn't take much from her. Think how much he'd had to take over the years. "It doesn't matter," he said. Painstakingly he kept a dead level tone of voice. "The truth is, I can't afford to handle you any more. But it doesn't matter."

"I know what you mean, you ain't got to pussyfoot. You've got this jail bond con and . . ." She was on the verge of hysteria, she might cry and cry. Oxie knew. Her voice bit like an auger into his hearing. She leaned and her distorted face came toward him, a face white and clenched and raw. She spat the words. "It makes you sick to the stomach, don't it, just to sit here with me?"

But she was wasting her time. He was once again in the plastic box, completely disconnected from her, completely aloof. "I offered you that ten spot, take it or leave it. As far as I'm concerned it's all finished."

"You can take that goddam money and ram it up your ass and tamp it down with a red-hot poker." She gasped for breath. "You can't shit me. You think you can treat me like one of these goddam Gimlet Street whores. I know who you are, buddy, and I know where you come from. You ain't no better than anybody else around here. You might have lucked up into a fast con or two, but you ain't no better than me. You ain't no different."

He smiled a sweetly sad smile. Forgiving. These words were the last words of Clemmie's that Oxie ever heard. He rose; shrugged slightly. "Clemmie," he said, "that's all there is. Take care of yourself."

He elbowed through the screen door and entered into the sunlight and turned right, going uphill on Rance Avenue. He was already giggling to himself and when he'd walked half a block he laughed outright. He laughed for almost a full minute. It wasn't all that funny; in fact, there was something a little sad, maybe a little lonesome, about the whole situation. But he was suffering a sensation of pure effervescent sweet relief and he had to laugh. Maybe he'd acted cruelly and maybe it wasn't right—he wasn't a cruel man. Even so, he couldn't stop his happiness and he laughed. If he had known that clipping loose from the girls would make him so happy he'd have done it long before.

Near the top of the hill, at the edge of the town square, he turned around and looked at the Gimlet Street neighborhood, lying before him in light and shadow, chopped into ruthless corners by streets and alleys. It was like looking back upon his own past history, and now of course it was no longer to be a part of his history. He gazed at the busy deceitful sleazy blocks thinking that in a few seconds, in just a moment, he would turn his back on this feverish gaudy place for good. He would have no connection, nothing there would ever touch his life again.

And somehow in his happiness was mixed an incomprehensible regret. A momentary complacent fondness for the place tugged at him.

He turned on his heel and walked into the square.

Hunger at last caught up with him; Oxie decided to have lunch. He might have eaten anyway, just to treat himself. He tooled his blue Buick all the way across town, not hurrying. At the Lamplighter House he ordered a medium rare New York Strip with onions and mushrooms, baked potato with sour cream and chives, a tossed salad with Lamplighter Special Dressing. The restaurant had a private club license and Oxie ordered set-ups and mixed himself a couple of drinks from the bottle in his own liquor locker.

He was the only customer in the place. His gaze moved lazily through the dimly lit room, over the dark wood-paneled walls, over the deep wine-colored carpet. He didn't break the luxurious mood by joking with the waitress; she came and went without speaking.

He ate enormously, enjoying the rich solitude. It was like being submerged in a magnificently appointed bathysphere. He was out of the world, untouchable, and he liked thinking of the people he knew and where they were at this moment. Jack Harloe was at McCabe's Body, grinding his ass to a fine powder over some undrivable heap of junk. Freene Sluder was sitting in his daddy's dusty law office with his feet on the desk, worrying, and waiting for the afternoon to die. Clemmie was either tying on a head-busting drunk or trying to pick up some blind john. Frankie Pickett—ha!—Frankie Pickett was in jail. It was as if he was thinking of a pack of wild dogs out there in a frozen flinty wilderness, each impotently scratching the ground.

He chewed his meat and thought. What would it be like to be very wealthy, wealthy so that you didn't have to puzzle about where it was coming from next week or next year? Floating through the world untouchable on a cushion of smooth money. Oxie frowned. It might not be as good as you'd think. The only truly rich people he'd ever encountered were a bunch of scrawny blue-haired old biddies; they each nagged a poor dumb husband into the grave, and then as soon as the first shovelful of dirt plopped down in his face, they set out to traipse the globe and spend the dump, giving the go eye to spick waiters and faggot bar piano players. He'd seen them haul out the restaurant manager, to tell him the soup wasn't hot or that the spoon wasn't clean

135

or the chicken wasn't young or that there was a frightening rain cloud in the northeast. . . . Well, okay. There might be danger in money for those kind of people, but you didn't have to be like that. You could keep cool; you didn't have to trade all your brains for money.

Not that all the disadvantages started at that level. For example: he had just finished his meal and now he wanted to pick his teeth. But it wasn't polite. Should he get up and go to the bathroom?

Oxie belched softly, covering his mouth with his napkin.

He checked his bright Tissot and signaled the waitress and asked for a telephone. He remembered the number. (A professional talent.)

"Mrs. Harper?" Oxie said.

"Yes."

"This is Ted Pape again. Is Mr. Harper in yet?"

"Just a moment, please."

He unwrapped a new cigar, sucked it and lit it.

"Hello?"

"Mr. Harper?"

"Yes."

"This is Ted Pape here. I wonder if I might arrange to meet you and have a talk with you if I could."

"I imagine so. I gather that this is rather important, Mr. Pape?"

"Yes sir, I believe it is. It concerns your son, Linn."

There came the unbelieving pause Oxie had expected.

"Linn? Linn? Is he all right? Has he been in an accident?"

"He's just fine, Mr. Harper. Perfectly safe. But he's got into a little trouble. . . ."

"But he *is* all right."

"Yes, he's fine."

"What kind of trouble?"

"Well, it's a little too complicated to go into over the phone. If we could arrange to meet . . ."

"You can't tell me what kind of trouble?"

136

"It's nothing really serious, I'm sure of that. But it is compli-cated and it might take me a little while to explain. I wonder if it would be all right to call on you at your home."

"Well, yes, if it concerns my son. You're certain that he's all right?"

"Perfectly safe and sound, Mr. Harper. Say I come to your house in half an hour?"

"That would be fine." Harper seemed to have calmed himself a bit. "Do you know where I live?"

"Yes. I took your address from the phone book." Oxie closed his eyes. "Fourteen fifty-three Wedgewood Drive."

"Yes, that's right. I'll see you in half an hour, then?"

"Yes sir," Oxie said. "I'll drive right over. Good-bye."

He hung up. Sat pondering. Harper seemed—over the tele-phone, anyway—to fit perfectly the idea Oxie had formed of him. Solid, educated and naggingly concerned about his kid. All that made simple sense. But he would have to take it easy. What would impress Harper? Manners, of course, and steadiness of de-meanor. Oxie signaled the waitress. If Jimmy Rogers, the man-ager of the Lamplighter, was in, he could borrow his car, a sweet new cream-colored Cadillac. Not that Oxie's Buick looked so bad; no, man, it looked damn fine. But he was going out to meet this Harper guy for the first time, and a Cadillac—well, it was just that much better.

It's a truth, and you can paste it on your shaving mirror: appearance is important. You got to put your best foot forward.

—Ah Oxie, Oxie. How come you do the things you do?

—Necessity, baby. Necessity pure and simple. What you would do if you were in my shoes. There's nothing weird about Theo-dore Pape.

—You're putting me on. Oxie, honey, you don't have to do anything. You've got it made already. How much do you need to have? What can a man do with it all?

—You may not believe it, but it's not going to stay like it is.

137

Nothing ever stays put. Take it from me, there's hard times coming. And if a man's got a chance to set things up, he goddam well better grab it.

—That's not the real reason, is it?

—I don't know. What's it to you?

—There's a lot of wise men who have thought about you. Guys with real brains and education and all kinds of resources. And they don't understand you an ounce. It's a fact, Oxie, that you're thoroughly unfathomable. What do you think about when you're putting on your underwear or emptying the ashtrays during a party or falling asleep at night? What do you dream of? I can't imagine what you think.

—I think about the money and the good-looking women.

—Sweetheart, you've already got the money and the good-looking women.

—I think about more of the same. . . . What the hell's eating you, anyhow? Why aren't you happy? This is a fine day, a beautiful day. And here we are riding in a big off-white Cadillac with air conditioning, just rolling down the avenue, and the johns on the sidewalk staring at us hungry. Maybe we won't live to see a day like this again.

Why don't you see if you can find us a good tune on the radio?

Just turn the button and set the dial.

Andrew Harper

Is there anyone who honestly considers himself a good parent?

Is there anyone who has a viable notion of what that phrase *good parent* means?

A man comes into your house to tell you that your son has been arrested and is at this moment behind bars. What's your reaction?

My reaction was to be attacked immediately by a thousand garish panic-stricken fantasies, pouring in my head like a river of fever dreams. Linn has robbed/ no, murdered someone/ he has been found a narcotics addict/a car wreck . . . An uncountable number of notions, bursting separately and vividly in my mind like a fireworks display.

Yet I had always supposed that I trusted Linn. He is first my son; and then he is intelligent, loyal and fair-minded. Besides our obvious relationships of love and blood, I'd felt another kinship between us, an abstract double allegiance to an idea of justice. It's true that we never talked about it—why for God's sake should we?—but it was nevertheless felt between us. At least, I felt it on my side.

So that when these fantasies ceased, went away as quickly as they came, my first physical impulse was to say to this Mr. Pape,

139

Horseshit, fellow, what's your game? But I choked it back and said, "Are you sure you've got the right family, Mr. Pape?"

"Yes sir, I am," he said. He had a low thick voice. Mushmouth is the local name for it. "I recognized his picture from the newspaper."

"Oh yes," I said. I remembered that well enough. YOUNG SKYLARKS LOOK TO FUTURE. There had been some family embarrassment about that. "Won't you sit down?"

"Thank you."

He handed me his hat, which I'd forgotten to ask for, and took a corner of the sofa.

"Can I get you a drink?"

"No thanks. It's a little too early for me."

I quite simply didn't like this guy. Dark man of middle height with an odd apprehensively smooth manner. Very well dressed, if your idea of style is Mod Tout. That's how I classified him: a gambler, and maybe on his own terms a successful man, but at this moment quite clearly out of his milieu. So much out of his accustomed framework, in fact, that he couldn't help generating around himself an atmosphere of nervous guilt. Though so far as I knew he had nothing to feel guilty about. I simply didn't like him.

I put his hat on the TV set. The hell with it.

"What has Linn been arrested for, Mr. Pape?"

"Well," he said, crossing his legs, "I haven't quite been able to find out yet, but I'm sure it's nothing serious."

"Why are you sure it's not serious?"

"They've got him in the tank. If it was serious, they'd've put him by himself. Also they don't know his name."

"Why not?"

"He wouldn't tell them."

"Don't they check identifications?"

"Yes, sure they do. He must not've had any on him."

"And how did you find out who he was?"

"Like I say, Mr. Harper, I recognized him from his picture in the paper. I couldn't remember his name right off, so I went and looked it up."

140

The shadow of an annoyed frown passed over his face. I was pushing him and he knew it. It was the fact that he realized what I was doing that broke down his brittle grammar. I could see him reaching to grip himself more steadily.

"And you didn't inform the police? I think they'd like to know."

"I'm sure they would. But I thought it might be important for you to know first."

"Of course. I appreciate that, Mr. Pape."

"Anyhow," he said, and uncrossed his legs and leaned forward with his elbows on his knees—beginning to fight back a little now—"anyhow, if they really wanted to know who he was, they could find out. It wouldn't be a whole lot of trouble for them."

"Oh, I have every confidence in our police force."

"Yeah." He leaned back heavily. "That's why I say it must not be such serious trouble. They could have found out."

"I understand," I said, and shut up. Waiting him out.

"I thought you'd want to know first. Like maybe you wouldn't want a whole lot of publicity. And maybe you'd want to get in touch with your lawyer on this matter and you could get a head start so maybe it wouldn't have to come to court. And I thought it might be you'd want to get him out of that place. Now I can arrange that for you. I've got powers of attorney and I'm allowed to visit prisoners for business purposes, and it might be that I—"

"You're telling me, Mr. Pape, that you're a bondsman by profession."

Now it was an open frown and his voice went sharply bitter. "It's a living. We ain't—we can't all be professors."

"That's true. I don't think all of us would want to be."

He became darkly deliberate. "Your son seems to me like a mighty fine young man. He's got manners and he's got brains. Don't you want to get him out? That tank's not a comfortable place, full of drunks and hard . . . street fighters."

"Yes, certainly I'd like for him to get out. But I'm not sure he wants to come out. He doesn't seem to act in that interest."

"I don't think he knows exactly what he *is* doing. Or maybe he just don't want to face up to you."

141

That startled me. The idea of my punishing Linn hadn't crossed my mind. I'd really never had much occasion to, and when I did it was a more or less spontaneous kind of thing, taking away temporarily the first "privilege" that occurred to me. It was nothing like this cold-blooded strategy Mr. Pape implied.

"I don't think Linn's frightened of me," I said. But it sounded weak.

"Well, Mr. Harper, it's up to you. I'm at your service, whatever you decide."

"What about the other boys?" I asked. "Terry and uh Don?"

"No other boys his age in there," he said. "Friends of his?"

"Yes."

We fell silent. I lit a cigarette and Mr. Pape took a cigar from his jacket pocket, hesitated a moment as if he might ask my permission, but then went ahead and opened it, mouthed and lit it. A blue-gray gush of smoke about his face. I stared at him through it: this dark block of a man who so obviously belonged in a universe of easy women, absurdly powerful cars, overpriced Scotch. I was grateful for his information—yes, of course—but I would have given money never to have met Mr. Pape.

"You say he's in good shape, he hasn't been injured?"

"He looks fine to me. The arresting officers and the night desk sergeant were off duty so I couldn't get all the information I wanted. . . . But yes, he looks okay. A little scared, maybe. Pretty confused."

"Yes. If I were in his place I'd be frightened out of my wits."

"Uh-huh."

More silence. He was such an imposing strange presence there on the sofa that I had the feeling he weighted the room on his side, tipped it over, and I had to fight not to slide toward him.

"Mr. Pape," I said finally, "I'm going to have to think this over. It's quite a surprise to me, as I'm sure you've realized. Certainly I want to get Linn out of there as soon as possible. As you say, it can't be very pleasant and I can't imagine that it's doing him any good. But I'm going to have to think it over and talk about it with my wife. And I'll have to make arrangements."

142

He rose slowly but easily. "Sure, I understand." He took out a slip of paper and a ballpoint pen. "You might want to get in touch with me before you go down there. Like I say, I've got a lot of contacts in that place." He scribbled on the paper and handed it to me. "This here's my telephone number and if I'm not there they'll know how to find me. Just give me a ring any time you want to go down. I'll be there at nine o'clock anyway."

I took it from him, glanced at it and absentmindedly turned the slip over.

Braves	Cardinals	1
Dodgers	Giants	1
Yankees	White Sox	2

A baseball tipsheet. I hadn't seen one for years, not since I was an undergraduate. My instincts about him were justified, at any rate. I gave him a look.

He actually blushed; that is, his dark face grew darker. And almost stammered—before he gripped himself tight, and said in a dead level voice, "That's right, Mr. Harper. I've been known to take a bet once in a while. You can check it out. I'm entered for my federal gambling stamp down at the capital."

"As you say, Mr. Pape, we can't all be professors."

We shook hands. I watched him go down the walk with an easy businesslike stride. He clambered into a big creamy Cadillac and drove away. It looked like a great pale shark ceaselessly cruising for nourishment.

Then I closed the door and stood in front of the blank dark panels. I was dazed, quite as much by the encounter as by the fact that Linn was in jail. The absence of the man engendered a feeling of relief—if he had stayed longer we might have Mistered each other to death. But now that he was gone my son's predicament was borne in upon me that much more heavily.

I tried to think.

Finally I went to the telephone in the hall, looked up the numbers and called the parents of Linn's friends, the Englishes and the Burges. Mrs. English and Mrs. Burge were surprised by my calls. We had never met, and since the boys weren't expected back yet the ladies didn't understand why I was asking. Had anything happened? Hadn't been any trouble, had there? No no, I said. I just wanted to get in touch with Linn about something that had come up. I didn't want to alarm them, and I couldn't very well say I'd received information that my son was in jail. I fabricated some evasive white lies and hung up as soon as I half-graciously could. From Mrs. Burge I learned that their weekend cabin had no telephone; so that even if the boys had wanted to contact us they couldn't have.

(I also found out that I was now mentally referring to Linn as "my son." I'd always spoken of him and thought of him as Linn.)

Now I would have to tell Katherine. I didn't want to. A man never wants to be the bearer of bad news, especially to his wife. And more than that. Something of a shade of guilt in my feelings. Not responsibility; and not the cliché reaction, Oh-God-where-did-we-fail-him. But something. The fear perhaps that my own muddied perceptions and not particularly admirable life had partially edged into Linn's life, that his fair clean chances had already been darkened occultly by his choice of sire.

How Katherine would receive the news I could guess only dimly. She is not hysterical or easily upset; she is not even overly protective of Linn. But hidden in her there is an accusatory streak, an old trouble between us. Maybe it was my faint anticipation of this part of her that contributed to my possession of half guilt. Today she hadn't been feeling well. Her hay fever, recurrent in spring and fall, had come on her, now coupled with a cold or maybe a mild influenza. She had spent most of the day upstairs in bed, leafing through glossy magazines full of beautiful houses.

(I once twitted her about them. "Wish books," I said. "No," she said, "surrealist fantasy books.")

I went to talk with her. Going down the hall toward the stairs, I passed Linn's room. The door was open. I turned and came back and stood looking in.

144

Were there secrets here I should know? Were there clues? Except for the cluttered desk and the rumpled center of the bed where he must have flung himself down momentarily, the room was in neat order. A room ideally boyish, yet curiously unboyish. In some ways rather academic, almost aseptic. Suspended by wires overhead hung a polished model of the Project Mercury rocket ship that had attained a brief measure of local fame by being included in a newspaper photograph. (The newspaper photo: that was how Mr. Pape had identified Linn. Odd. Didn't seem the kind of thing that guy would hold in his mind.) The shelves were jammed and every level surface littered with lurid pulp magazines and paperback science fiction novels. Most of the names were as unfamiliar to me as Hungarian: Jack Williamson, August Derleth, *Venus Equilateral, The Dunwich Horror,* E. E. Smith, Ph.D. (What kind of guy actually signs his books Ph.D.?) And others familiar to me: H. G. Wells, Will Durant, *Thus Spake Zarathustra, Of Mice and Men,* Camus. A closely detailed National Geographic map of the moon was pinned to the wall above his desk.

With some trepidation I opened a desk drawer. What was I expecting? Pills? Pornography? Love letters? I think I expected exactly what, with an edge of disappointment, I found. Pencils, ruler, compass, eraser, paper clips. A single secret only: he had hoarded away six clippings of the newspaper article about himself. There were notes quite neatly set down on note cards in awkward script, mostly book titles or scientific jottings. A couple of books of matches.

In short, nothing. Or nothing anyway that gave me information I hadn't already known. Linn spent long hours here at his desk, but I could discover nothing unhealthily intriguing. Rather a professional desk. Not so very much different from my own. Almost idly I opened a novel by Clifford D. Simak and read, "They still believe in an ancient legend which says their race arose as the result of immigrants from another galaxy who landed on the rim and worked their way inward over many galactic years. They think that if they can get out to the rim they can turn that legend into history to their greater glory." No information here either, except for the fact that it was a much different sort of prose from what I was used to reading.

I thought about that. Should I have been showing all along more interest in Linn's hobbies, should I have tried to become his partner in these recondite pursuits? No dice. One knows better instinctively. He would only feel that he was being crowded. He had set out to create for himself a personality, an intellectual stance. Much interest on my part would threaten him.

I turned and came away, somewhat ashamed of myself. If he really had any secrets I didn't want to know them. The hardest people to keep secrets from are the members of your family, those who most importantly should be kept ignorant.

At the door I looked back and surveyed the room again. Because I *had* found out something; or, rather, I had renewed a former knowledge: that Linn did have a life sharply apart from my own, that he was continually making choices the importance of which I could not gauge, that as the distance between our characters widened our bonds of affection and respect strengthened. Maybe that's the hardest thing for me as a parent (and certainly not as a "good parent") to comprehend, that my affection for Linn would become queasier and more flaccid as my respect for him decreased. And that I had respect for him proportionate to his identity as a person separate from me. I doubt if this realization comes up to the mark as a piece of blinding wisdom, yet for me it's hard to keep continually in mind. What obscures it is the fact that our children are dependent upon us, if only circumstantially so. I have a love for the music of Sibelius. If I am to keep Linn in hamburgers and blue jeans, isn't it only fair that he spend what time he can listening to and reading about Sibelius?

(Turns out of course that he digs Miles Davis and John Coltrane.)

And he was perhaps never so urgently dependent upon me than at this moment, clapped into jail, scared and bewildered. Yet

146

still maintaining the person he conceived he was, independent in his own terms, refusing to divulge his name and address.

I leaned against the jamb and took out my handkerchief, noticing that it wasn't any too fresh. I used it to snuff away the hard little tears at the corners of my eyes.

I went down the hall and up the stairs, slowly and deliberately. For some reason I kept my eyes on my feet and I thought, One step at a time. Why had I been projecting Linn's emotions? It was I who was confused and bewildered.

Katherine was sitting in bed, her back propped up by pillows, the bedclothes drawn midway up her chest.

"How are you feeling?" I asked.

"Stuffy and uncomfortable," she said, "but not absolutely miserable. What was your mysterious caller all about? I heard him come in and leave, but I was too lazy to get up and eavesdrop."

I pulled the sewing chair away from the cosmetics table and sat.

She looked at me expectantly, raising her eyebrows. She was lying, with her arms out of the sheets, amid a scatter of beautiful-house magazines whose glossy covers reflected the sunlight in glaring patches. Even with her nose red and her cheeks flushed, and even after eighteen years, she looked as far as I was concerned quite beautiful. A long smooth milky neck that would have hypnotized Modigliani; brave, almost masculine, shoulders; slim and thin hands which did not show veins on the backs. She stretched her legs beneath the sheets and I visualized them, long and well turned and glowingly white, almost luminous. She kept herself in shape; the most she ever weighed was, I think, 120 pounds. Well, she had something worth taking care of.

I sighed.

"What's the matter? Something's wrong, isn't it?"

"I'm afraid so."

"Well, what? You're the most exasperating man."

"I was trying to figure out some easy way to tell you. . . . Linn's in jail."

"No, what is it? You always have to kid around."

"Katherine, I'm telling you the truth. He really is in jail."

She looked utterly astonished, and maybe not quite believing me even yet, though surely she could read my face by now.

"My God. What happened? Is he all right? He hasn't been hurt, has he? My God."

"From what I can gather, he's okay. I wish I knew more about it."

I told her what I had heard just as I'd heard it, except that I included a mostly fanciful and not very flattering character sketch of Mr. Pape. I watched her changing expressions. She didn't seem to have been attacked by fearful fantasies as I had been. In fact, she took in the whole situation calmly and with a kind of passionate equanimity, nodding her head vigorously whenever I would drop a remark pointing out a detail that might possibly accrue to Linn's favor. There weren't many of these, but Katherine seemed solidly satisfied about them. I must admit that neither of us showed any concern for whatever might be the abstract justice of the incident. But where I had been assaulted by doubts—self-doubts more than anything else—Katherine seemed to have none at all. Motherly love and all that, was my first reaction. But I caught something else in her expressions of satisfaction, just a peep of another thinking voice. Amid everything else it was for her also a matter of family pride.

I thought, Oh my God no. Oh Jesus no.

At last I finished, and she lay thinking quietly for a moment.

"That's all I know," I said. "That's all our riverboat gambler told me."

"Well, for the moment it's quite enough," she said. And smiled.

That threw me. I hadn't expected hysteria or any kind of corny "womanly" breakdown. But neither had I expected this smooth imperturbability, the smiling confidence. She'd obviously thought of something I hadn't.

"More than enough," I said. "What are you grinning about?"

"I'm not grinning, I'm merely smiling. Trying to reassure you,

148

if you must know. You really look awful, scared and haggard."

"I never was good at hiding my feelings."

"No, you never were."

"Well . . ." I put my hands on my knees as if to get up.

"What are you going to do?"

"I'm going to see what I can do about getting Linn out and bringing him home."

"How are you going to do that?"

I sank back into the too-small chair. "I hadn't thought about it in any detail. I suppose I should go down there and identify myself and ask to see him. After I've talked to him I'll know more about what I can do."

"You don't know any of those people down there."

"No I don't. But they are policemen, after all. I imagine they'll be glad to find out who Linn is, since he hasn't been telling them. I imagine they'll be happy to talk to his father."

She moved her long legs restlessly under the sheets. "That's what you imagine, but you don't know. Those people down there, they're a race apart. At least in a little old mountain town like Braceboro, they are. It's not only policemen down there you have to talk to. The policemen can't do anything by themselves. It's always somebody else. It's better if you know somebody they know."

"Like who?" I asked, praying she wouldn't say the name I knew she was going to.

"Like Uncle Zeb," she said firmly.

"Jesus God on a popsicle, Katherine."

"I'm serious," she said.

All this is perhaps not hard for other people to understand. But it's hard for me; and what I do understand of it, I detest. Detest almost automatically, and maybe react against too violently and quickly and unreasonably. But I can't help that— something goes against the grain of your personality and what you hope at least are your convictions, and you respond almost helplessly, reflexively. (And wasn't it possible Linn also reacted

149

in the same manner? He too had now occupied some time in building his convictions.)

What I have in mind is the fact that in the mountains of western North Carolina there are several severe and clearly delineated social castes. This is not exactly what one could call a novelty, right? But when you consider what American social prestige is built upon, money first of all and then family history, you have to stand amazed that the idea of social classes ever took root in these hills. There's no money, or anyway nothing that would be considered *real* money by an even moderately successful New Jersey lawyer or Mississippi planter or California real estate dealer. The terrain simply doesn't lend itself to extensive cultivation, a great deal of the land standing in a well-nigh vertical position; and since the economy is still almost entirely agrarian, the possibilities of a fortune in crops are tightly restricted. And it is a result of historical circumstance that landholdings by individuals are modest indeed. In Alabama a man's "fair-sized farm" may cover upwards of twenty thousand acres; in the Carolina mountains two hundred acres in one piece make up a pretty large holding. (It is by no means an uncommon occurrence for mountain farmers to kill each other off in shotgun battles over boundary disputes involving fences no more than a foot and a half out of line. The property deeds section of the county courthouse can offer up histories of whole bloody Antietams and Chickamaugas.) Add to these two facts one more: the climate and terrain preclude the growing of most southern money crops; no cotton, no peanuts, peaches, soybeans. (A "money crop" is what you can sell at harvest for honest-to-God cash money.) There is burley tobacco and there is wintered beef and there is some amount of varied truck farming; and except for apples in a few counties and maybe beans and gladioli in a couple of others, that's just about all there is.

So much for money and its social caste.

As for illustrious family histories, any pedigreed redbone hound dog can beat most of them all hollow. True enough, that a number of families have been here a long time. Smatherses, Burnettes, Boones, Fergusons have been digging themselves into the coves and creeks and rocks ever since the first white men got themselves lost in these shadowy laurel thickets. But about all they ever achieved was to raise brood after brood of sullen yellow-haired children and to hold on fiercely and meanly to every stony, reasonably level field they could attach themselves to. While it's true, as the etymologists and folklorists so solemnly aver, that in these parts you can still hear traces of Elizabethan conversational language (*clomb* for *climbed* and the like), it is equally true that no Christopher Marlowe or Michael Drayton will ever be nurtured here. What there was of a native culture, mostly dreary folk ballads and raw square dance tunes, has eagerly surrendered to the omnipresent sound of radio and television. Of the political philosophy, what can one say? Reactionary without discernible tradition, racist without even a visual trigger (Negro people are scarce), opportunist without much hope of reward. Local politics, I mean; the presence of mountaineers in statewide politics is next to nil. You can count on two or three lonely fingers the number of state governors from hill country. (The town of Braceboro has for a navel the statue of one of them, Zebulon Johns. A big green thing, faithfully rendered in the style of Nineteenth-Century Awful.) The geographical isolation and the sparse population of the western counties account for this fact, of course; but it also insures that any local society belle must tally up for forebears a long grim line of snuff-dippers, tobacco-spitters, coon-hunters and bootleggers. Not that our unblushing beauty would be averse to this. These are the people she calls Family, and she's likely to take a weird pride in counting among her uncles and in-laws a couple of violent drunkards and psychotic dog-poisoners.

Up here they use the word in just that way, a bare defiant tri-syllable: Family. So-and-so comes from Family, they say; or, Yes, but old Jim has Family. Anywhere else in the South you'll hear, Well, he comes from a good family. Or maybe you'll even hear that he comes from good stock. But in the mountains it's Family. Period.

My wife, Katherine, comes from Family.

151

I didn't know this when I met her, and even by the time we got married I'd understood very little about it. There wasn't much chance for me to know. When we met she was an undergraduate and I was working on my doctorate at a Tennessee university. The only times I met her family were during holiday trips to her home, brief and hectic stays, clamorous with an exhausting hospitality I was always relieved to get away from. After graduate school I'd taken teaching positions in Missouri and Arkansas, so that sojourns among her kinsmen became even more infrequent.

Opportunities to know her family were complicated by the fact that I too was born in North Carolina, but in the mideastern part of the state; and when we visited our respective families for a couple of weeks every two or three years during summer vacations we went separately. In sixteen years of marriage I doubt I'd spent a total of three weeks' time with her folks. But two years ago a position was offered me here at William Watson College. The money was fairly good, and since Katherine had been complaining mildly of homesickness for a number of years, I decided to take it.

Why not? For me one place to teach is pretty much the same as another, and it was an opportunity for Katherine to return to the place she'd been brought up and for which she'd evinced a murmurous fondness over fifteen solid years. Happy years mostly, though not conspicuously prosperous. From what little I knew of her family there seemed no reason to suppose I shouldn't get along with them quite easily. And in my last few years at Arkansas it had occurred to me that Linn had no real experience of family traditions, he had in a sense no roots.

I would have preferred—selfishly, of course—to move to the eastern part of Carolina, near my own kin, but the job offer didn't come from that area. Supposing that, so far as Linn was concerned, one side of his genealogy was as good as another, I brought us here. Linn was satisfied and Katherine bloomed happily.

Well, it's different here. As I say, I knew nothing at all about the crazy local caste system. I come from a farm family too, a large one. (Seven brothers and four sisters I counted.) What the exact social position of my own family was, I'd never considered. Hell, it was good enough for me. We're gentle people; hardly what you'd call genteel, but anyhow honorable and industrious. And always among us a solid respect for a college education, legacy from my father, who died in his fifties. All twelve of us wound up with a college degree of one sort or another.

Nothing to be ashamed of, so far as I can see. Katherine must have thought so, for long ago I had courted her and married her without a word between us concerning social position, without recognition on my part of any difference. But a couple of weeks after we'd moved here to the mountains my education commenced.

It was at a Sunday Family dinner at the Mackie Farm, some forty miles west of Braceboro. When I asked Katherine the nature of the affair, she said, "Oh, it's just the Sunday dinner that Uncle Zeb likes to have every year."

"Uncle Zeb?"

"Zebulon Johns Mackie." That was how she called him: all three names, like a woman poet of the 1920's. And without apparent irony.

"Your mother's side of the family?"

"Well, obviously." She laughed.

"Any kin to our historically illustrious governor? Or just named after him?"

"Kin," she said. "You hear a lot about that. Mama's family is full of Johnses."

"Well, I'm mightily impressed. Should I be?"

"I don't know," she said. "Maybe not. He tries to put on the old-country-boy thing a little too much. . . . But you'll probably like him. Everybody does."

And of course I did. One could hardly help it, because at first sight he was a dead ringer for Benjamin Franklin. Not the real historical Ben Franklin, of course, for even though (or maybe because) I spend my life in the study of history, the physical ap-

153

pearances of historical personages of earlier centuries I cannot adequately imagine. Not enough to try to describe. (Though like everyone else, I have private and hidden images of some figures. I once tried to draw my fantasy-picture of James I. Ha.) But Uncle Zeb had the face of the Benjamin Franklin that every fairly literate American of a certain period carries in his head. The *Saturday Evening Post,* Norman Rockwell face: the fatherly spectacles, the head nobly bald with a patrician fringe, gravure of lines at cheek and eye indicating geniality, humor, sturdy common sense. Etc. Throw in your own list of soppy adjectives. I can go on longer about this, but maybe it's simpler and clearer just to say that this was the first guy I ever met who could accurately be described as *beaming.*

There he stood in the large dining room, sunny and airy, of the Mackie farmhouse. He'd got rid of his coat, and his otherwise gleaming white stiff shirt front was gray with sweat at armpit and collar and belt bulge. He was paunchy and pink enough, but he didn't look soft. He stood making loud jokes among his darker and rawer kinsmen, while one of a number of sallow teen-aged nieces "fixed him a plate" from the long table groaning with piles of baked ham and country ham, heaps of fried chicken, rice, sweet potatoes, bowls of sawmill gravy, sliced tomatoes and cucumbers, boiled corn, buttermilk biscuits—that almost savage cornucopia of food they're pleased to call Plain Country Cooking. When the girl brought him the staggering plateful, so shy and deferential she wouldn't look into his face but stared steadfastly at the highly polished toes of his old-fashioned black shoes, he joked and patted her on the head. I swear he did. I saw it.

But as I say, I liked him. We'd never met, but he recognized me on sight, knew me well enough to begin by calling me by my first name. Didn't quite punch me on the arm, but he might have without surprising me.

"Well, Andrew," he said, "I hear that you're quite the scholar."

"I'm a history teacher," I said. "But not so much a scholar, I'm afraid."

154

"That's not the way I hear it." He swallowed down a spoonful (that's right, a spoonful) of rice and gravy, picked up a chicken breast and bit into it. A white string of flesh fluttered at the corner of his mouth. "I hear you're a real smart scholar, write books and all."

"Not really." I'd published one short obscure article on Sir Walter Ralegh.

"Our Family never has been blessed with many scholars. Not real scholars like you. Course now, we've most of us got down a pretty fair amount of school-learning and book-learning. When I went off to college, why, I delved right into history myself. But there didn't seem much a feller could *do* with it. Go out and *do* something, if you know what I mean. So after college I went into law school. But I never regretted a minute I put into studying history. No sir. And not a minute I spent on my Latin, either. I found out in law school that I was a jump ahead of them other fellers. You know, with the consuls and proconsuls and the aediles and Justinian and all."

"It's a good background for any number of professions," I said bravely. But I could feel the ground turning to jello beneath me.

"Of course it is. Even if it wasn't it'd behoove a man to know these things." (In less than a minute of conversation, he'd used the words *delve* and *behoove*. By now I knew he'd season them with *feller* and *ain't*.) "It's the trouble with people today, and I include your high and mighty politicians too. Nobody knows their history any more. Not nearly as good as they ought to. People just don't care about the old things any more."

"I'm afraid you're right."

"Now you take how many years it's been since I studied my history in school. Longer than I care to think about, I can say that much. But I've never lost interest. And I'll tell you a secret: I'm still carrying on a little research of my own. I've got a little old project I'm studying up on."

"Oh?"

Oh . . .

"I don't guess it'll seem like much to you, considering what you're interested in. England and all, I mean. What I've been doing is more like local history. I been thinking about making a history of Bunker County, our own county here. I've already put a lot of things down on paper. I suppose there's folks would turn up their noses at it and say it's not real history at all. Not important kind of history, no kings or proconsuls or anything. But it's actually very interesting. A lot of interesting things have been done in this county. Some Civil War battles, and laying the narrow gauge railroad through, and the Challenger Paper Company. Things like that. A lot of it I don't even have to look up. Part of our Family history, you know."

"Yes."

"When I was a boy, why, I didn't like nothing better than to set on the porch and listen to the old folks go on about how things used to be. Trouble today is, young folks don't pay the old folks no mind. Think they know it all already."

"It sounds very interesting."

"Well, it is." He leaned and—finally—did punch me on the arm. "You and me ought to get together. I've got the material. What I ain't got down on paper I've got up here in the old punkin. Now, with the way you know how to write and do the proper kind of research, and with what I know and the information I can get hold of . . . Well, it seems to me like we ought to be able to cook up a mighty fine volume, you and me."

As Joe Louis said of the Billy Conn match, there was no place to hide. "It might take a long while," I said. "I really don't have the kind of free time I need for this sort of thing. It would probably take a few years to verify the materials."

"Oh yes," he said. "We'd have to take our time. We don't want nothing shoddy."

That was that.

Katherine and I talked about it as we drove back home. But she treated the matter lightly, obviously not sharing my cold horror.

156

"It's just a fancy he has," she said. "He really doesn't expect anything to come of it."

I put on a gloomy voice. "You just wait. There'll be a thirty-pound manuscript in the mailbox tomorrow."

She laughed. "Hardly. Uncle Zeb never wrote down a hundred words in a row in his life. Even as a lawyer, he gets other people to do that kind of thing for him."

"All the worse. That means he'll send me a bunch of maundering garbage he's dictated at odd moments."

"It doesn't have to be garbage." Quick burn of anger in her voice.

"No no," I said. "Don't get me wrong. Nothing against the old gentleman. It's just that he's an amateur historian obsessed with a not very interesting subject."

"Why is it not interesting?"

I could feel an argument developing. My fault too, because I couldn't find any tactful words to explain the sheer dread in me. "Well, of course, it's interesting in its own right. But there are other subjects that have first claim on one's attention."

"Oh really? Don't you remember what you said? You once told me that one of the reasons you were attracted to history was because it was equalitarian. You said, if one could see them in an impartial light, every event would weigh equally with every other."

"Laying the narrow gauge railroad through Balsam Gap. For Christ's sake."

"It connected us with the rest of the state. With the rest of the country. There weren't any roads then."

When she said that, I could feel curtains peeling back in my mind, the folding back of curtains revealing windows on whole landscapes of Katherine's personality. Things I had never seen. I'd known her for seventeen years, we'd been married for sixteen; but for the first time I discovered that my wife was pure Mountain and ferociously Family. It was good to know. I felt a new kind of tenderness toward her.

157

"You're pretty damn snobbish, you know that?" she said.

"I'm finding out you're right," I said, "but I'm trying to fight it."

But then it turned out I was more nearly correct than Katherine was. Uncle Zeb's manuscript arrived the following Friday and it surpassed even my fears about it. Names, dates, truncated anecdotes, gnomic jottings, inchoate thoughts on every conceivable kind of scrap paper, including laundry lists and stock feed bills. And old letters from unidentified correspondents and newspaper clippings and eight mimeographed pages of newsletter from when Uncle Zeb had been "official journalist" on Kiwanis jaunts to Jerusalem and Las Vegas. These had been written in a deliberately illiterate Sut Lovingood style designed, so far as I could discover, to hint at but not illuminate the drunken peccadilloes of his fellow pilgrims. And other notes whose purposes and meanings I could not even guess at.

It had been not mailed but delivered in a Schenley whiskey carton by one of Uncle Zeb's flunkies, a tubercular-looking farmer. I took it into the kitchen for Katherine to have a look at. She was sitting on a stool at the breakfast bar, penciling a correction into *The Joy of Cooking.*

"What in the world is that?" she asked.

"This," I said, "is *The Johns-Mackie History of Bunker County.* In raw form, of course."

"Raw is the word. It doesn't even look unearthed."

"Oh well," I said. "I'll just have to dig if I'm going to get down to the veins of pure gold."

"I suppose. What *are* you going to do with that?"

"What, indeed. I was hoping you could tell me."

"*I* could tell? You're the historian. You're the one who's so all-fired smart about them kings and proconsuls."

"Come on, wifey. Give me a break."

"What do you want me to do?"

"I want you to call your uncle and get me off the hook."

"How am I to do that? What am I supposed to tell him?"

"Tell him that the mere sight of it has driven me stark staring

158

insane. Tell him I'm suddenly down with terminal cancer. Tell him I've got a job with the FBI, posing as a headhunter in Borneo."

"Which?"

"It doesn't matter. They'll all come true before I try to handle this box of goodies."

"I don't think I will," she said. "You got yourself into this, or at least let yourself get into it. You'll have to get out by yourself."

"That's not quite fair. I was just trying to be nice to your uncle. After all, that was the first time I'd met your family in its native state and habitat."

"You seemed to like him well enough at the time."

"I liked him fine. But how was I to know he was going to do *this* to me?" I must have sounded more querulous than usual because she once more started to take offense.

"There's no point in making such a melodrama of it. It's certainly nothing so very serious. You make it sound like he was some sort of gangster. He's just an old man with some fond notions."

"Yes. I wish he was a gangster instead. I wish he was an unlettered safecracker."

Later of course I found out that nice old Uncle Zeb was a gangster.

This information I came upon more or less accidentally. And though it was Katherine who dropped the remark that enabled me to put it all together I never told her what I knew, preferring —wisely, I thought, for once in my life—to keep my own counsel.

So far as corruption goes, Uncle Zeb's achievement was really nothing special. Enormously profitable, no doubt, but not truly imaginative. I had been following the story in the paper, in the second section devoted to local news, for something over a year. The swindle was so simple and obvious on the face of it that it could actually be pieced together for the most part simply by reading the news stories.

The Braceboro city government had decided, quite justly it

was agreed, that the town was badly in need of a large municipal parking lot. The city council, of which Katherine's uncle was an esteemed and loudly oratorical member, ordered that the proposal be included in a popular referendum entailing among other things an extension of the outmoded sewage system and a school bond issue. Every proposal on the referendum passed quite handily, probably because mountain people are known almost never to vote against anything involving the well-being of public schools. They have the unquestioning respect toward public education that many people in economically deprived areas have. One of their favorite parabolic examples is the capsule career of So-and-So who didn't have much of a family but who studied hard and did well in school and went off to college and got to be a dentist or engineer and came back to the mountains and Made Good. This person represented their most common type of folk hero, and among his other heroic attributes were the abilities to spell right off the bat any word you cared to utter and to multiply numbers and add enormous sums immediately, "all in his head, without even taking out a pencil."

So the referendum passed and the municipal parking lot was approved. It was envisaged not as the modern kind, one of those gray concrete wedding-cake affairs where you drive your car dizzily round and round an internal corkscrew, but simply as an asphalt parking lot with white stripes and parking meters. This lot was to be located near the center of town, smack in the middle of what the newspapers referred to as "the Gimlet Street section." A sensible idea, really. The place was an eyesore, a down-at-heels area consisting, so far as I could tell when driving by, of beer joints, whorehouses, gambling shops and so forth. It thrived on what money it could scavenge from the pockets of soldiers laying over for bus connections and from the truck farmers who sold their produce in the open-air market at the northern edge of the area. Of course, the most profitable season for the place was during the months of November and December when the farmers brought their burley tobacco to the Braceboro warehouses for auction.

160

A municipal parking lot would undoubtedly improve Gimlet Street. In the first place, the street would become more widely public, so that laws and ordinances would be more strictly enforced. And because of the welcome convenience of the parking lot the larger businesses would move in, the supermarkets and department stores and chain short-order restaurants. Not that the entertainments that made Gimlet Street famous would suddenly cease to be. Hardly. They were too deeply rooted in the economic and cultural life of the town. But they would be forced to remove to less central parts of the city. They would become less obvious.

Bids on the construction of the parking lot were turned in, and a company called Green Ridge Construction came up with the lowest. So far, everything straightforward. But because of prior commitments to other projects this company was not able to begin work immediately, and a beginning date some six months later was announced. No money was put down by either side. The city didn't even buy the property for the project. The value was, however, depressed, for it was obvious that when the city did decide to make its move, it would simply condemn the area and pick up the land at a nearly nominal price.

In the interim it was announced in the paper that Z. J. Mackie, good old Uncle Zeb, had bought himself a large slice of this soon-to-be-condemned property at the current going rate. My first thought when I read it was—honest to God—that the paunchy old gentleman had at last fallen victim to dotage. If my naiveté seems excessive I can only answer that it probably was. And still is, in most matters of this sort. What the hell reason could he have for buying, except in a fit of idiocy? For though it seemed a bargain compared with other real estate prices, and was certainly a bargain compared with its former estimate of worth, there was no chance of selling it to the city for a profit, no matter if Uncle Zeb was a council member. If he'd been mayor he couldn't have cranked a profit out of it, for no matter how cheaply he acquired it on the open market the price was going to be much lower once the city condemned the property.

161

When I read of his acquisition I couldn't help having a bit of a giggle, and after that feeling rather sorry for him. No doubt he could afford to lose the money, but surely it must hurt his pride. Another unspoken part of the local code of Family was that to remain a member in good standing one had continually to show himself as a razor-sharp horse trader. (This requirement belonged to the grand unwritten Philosophy of Common Sense, a set of tenets quite often seemingly at odds with the Philosophy of the Value of a Good Education.) (But this notion of horse trading as a prerequisite for sterling character may actually have been no more than a form of creeping Yankeeism; I don't think it would apply so thoroughly in the deeper South, in New Orleans or Mississippi, where it is permissible to admire a temperamental ineptitude in matters of business.)

A new development of the affair transformed my wondering naiveté into black suspicion. The papers announced that a new site for the parking lot was being considered. And then that it had been approved. On the face of it, the reasons for choosing another site were sound and reasonable. For one thing, it was discovered that the originally proposed site was one of the sections centrally involved with the expansion of the sewage system. Much digging and laying of pipe and installing of equipment, so that the parking lot would be long and inconveniently delayed. A second, and more clearly compelling, reason for the change was that another suitable piece of property, though it was not quite so close to the main square, could be got by the city for considerably less money than the Gimlet Street area was going to cost. So that it looked to a concerned citizenry—if there was such—that our city council was both perspicacious and frugal.

As indeed they were, if Uncle Zeb was an accurate index. For he had managed cheaply to pick up a large slice of property that for all its sleaziness and troublesomeness had to be enormously profitable in terms of leases and rents. Even so, I might have thought that he'd just been lucky if I hadn't had to keep remembering that after all he *was* on the city council. God knows how

162

many hours of heavy paternalism and arm-punching and what a long list of whiskey promises it took to put over this deal. The estimate was dizzying. Or sickening.

I didn't tell Katherine what I'd found out. I hadn't even known whether she'd been keeping up with the matter as it had been reported. Turned out she hadn't. I dropped the remark that it looked like Green Ridge Construction wouldn't be working on Gimlet Street after all, but over on the south side of town instead.

She didn't show much interest. "Oh?"

"They've found a more suitable site, they say."

"I'm afraid I haven't been keeping up with it. But it'll make Uncle Zeb happy, I suppose."

"Why is that?"

"It'll give his company a contract, won't it? He's on the board of directors for Green Ridge."

"Oh. I see."

I saw.

(Later I also found out that Safeway Sanitary Engineering Corporation, which won the contract for sewage expansion, was a subsidiary company of Green Ridge Construction. That made at least three ways Uncle Zeb was getting money out of this single bond issue, and by now I was willing to bet that there were a dozen others. He was enjoying a very remunerative dotage.)

But, as I say, I'd never told Katherine what I'd found out, so that my reluctance to enlist Uncle Zeb's aid in retrieving our son from the blue grasp of the law must have struck her as unreasonable, if not downright demented. Or maybe only as childish.

"I'm not joking," she said. "Those people down at the jailhouse really are a different breed. To them, you're just a schoolteacher, and they're not going to listen to you. But they know who Uncle Zeb is, and they will pay him some attention."

"You're probably right. Uncle Zeb's a different breed all by himself. I just don't want to ask him."

"You're still embarrassed about his project."

"Project?" Had she found out about the swindle?

"Don't tell me you've already forgotten that brilliant joint history of Bunker County."

"Oh. That." I hadn't forgotten, though I'd surely put enough energy into trying to. Still in its whiskey carton, the bundle of weird data awaited me beneath the basement steps. "No, I haven't forgotten."

"But you haven't done anything with it."

"Well, I've sort of filed it."

"You mean, you've put it where you don't have to look at it."

"Yes."

"And now you're ashamed to ask for help from him because you haven't done what you promised."

"Well, that's not exactly the reason."

"What is it then?"

I was debating whether to tell her about the Big Caper. Finally I didn't. I was curious—I still remain curious—about what her reaction would be, but in the instances his name had come up between us she had been so eager to come to his defense that I felt I would embroil myself in a fruitless and (as Linn was at this moment suffering God knows what inner turmoil) irrelevant argument. Besides, to be honest, Katherine was partly right; I did harbor some guilt about that county history. I not only hadn't done anything about it; I hadn't even contacted the old fraud.

"I'd just rather not," I said. "It doesn't seem quite kosher somehow."

"My, you certainly are the high-minded idealist today, aren't you? But you know, I'm not entirely sure Linn would appreciate your motives. I'm quite certain I don't." She took the telephone directory from a shelf of the night stand and opened it in her lap and began leafing through the yellow pages.

She'd put her finger deftly upon the place where she and I differed. I was certain that if Linn possessed what information I had, he'd spend any amount of time in jail rather than depend upon the influence of an uncle whose machinations he could not help consider shocking. Maybe it's a difference between men and women, or anyhow between mothers and fathers. Mothers often

164

seem more reluctant than fathers to let go their children, to allow them scope for self-determination—because they are less able to comprehend on the part of the offspring any loyalty to ideas, that loyalty to an idea which is in large part one of the wellsprings of individual personality. In her role as mother at least the female is blessed, or cursed, with a minuscule degree of detachment. Whatever it was, I knew surely that Linn would be ashamed that family influence was used in his behalf.

Katherine lifted the white telephone into her lap and began to dial.

I got up and left the room. I didn't want to hear the words she was going to say. I could guess them well enough to know that I would burn with shame and become bitterly angry. In fact, that was the way I felt already, and betraying my emotions to Katherine would only aggravate them.

I went downstairs into the kitchen and got the ice tray from the refrigerator and ran some water over it, but not enough, because I gashed my thumb lifting the sharp underedge of the lever. I swore for a while, wrapped the dish towel around my thumb, rinsed the blood off most of the ice cubes and made a rigorous bourbon and water. Gulped it down before it had a chance to get cool and poured another, rather less explosive this time, and stood drinking it at the pink-stained sink, looking out the window.

My tensions were momentarily relieved a little, as much from the minor bloodletting as from the whiskey. Should I attempt to describe my own temperament? Seems not much point in it since the degree of truth would be nearly impossible to determine. But maybe it's helpful to know that I consider myself an emotionally quiet person. Not that my feelings aren't strong or deep: I happen to believe that they are. But each feeling is usually single; the only way I have been able to establish even momentary emotional certainties for myself (shoring up against a relentless and professional intellectual skepticism) is to offer my mind completely to whatever feeling appears strongest. Ambiguous emotions are rare. . . . But today I'd been attacked by a plethora of feelings and fantasies amid which I was totally lost.

165

Worst of all was my recognition of the necessity of the situation. Uncle Zeb had to be called into it, and that was that. It was the single necessity of the fact that made me feel so rebelliously frustrated. For though I demand in personal dilemmas emotional singleness, I also demand latitude of action, wider possibilities of solution than generally offer themselves. One of the horrors of reading history is to watch those reported events march upon the pages, strident, martial, antlike, as if there were some absolutely compelling reason for things to have taken place in the stupid manner they have done. I can hardly read a biography without wanting to shout out to the central figure, Don't do that, do this instead! But when you get to page 400 they've committed the idiocies you knew they were going to, and they go down clutching desperately at the frayed rope end of a destiny usually too weak to succor them or even give them the cold comfort of a dignified conclusion. *If push comes to shove* is the colloquial phrase that for me expresses the finest point of our historical tragedy: humanity helpless because choice is absent.

Now I sipped my third (and weakest) bourbon, looking through the kitchen window at the afternoon growing dim while finches and sparrows jumped about ferociously in the pale green frilly new leaves of a maple. Upstairs Katherine was entering into dreadful collusion with her uncle, and Linn and I were betrayed helplessly and ignorantly. At last I heard her calling me and I went into the bathroom and clapped a Band-Aid on my thumb and once more climbed the stairs to the bedroom.

It was very dim now in the room and I turned on the lamps on the dresser and the night stand.

"What happened to your thumb?" Katherine asked.

"I cut it."

She reddened even through her illness. "Honestly, Andrew, sometimes you make me so angry I think I'll burst."

"Why?" I seemed to have lost track completely. Then: "Oh . . . I cut myself on the ice tray, trying to make a drink. It's nothing."

"You're pretty close to helpless, you know that?"

"That's why I married a hard-nosed woman," I said. "Well,

what's the word? Has Uncle Z. consented to solve all our problems forever?"

"There's no reason to be snotty. He doesn't have to do a damn thing, you know."

"I'd just about take a bet that you're wrong," I said. "My thought is, that once he'd heard about it, a personal edict from God wouldn't stop him from poking in."

"He was asked to. We asked him to."

"One of us did."

"For God's sake, Andrew."

"Okay. Okay, I'm sorry. What's happening now? What kind of rabbit does he have up his sleeve?"

"He's making a few calls and after that he's coming by to pick you up. You-all can go down to the police station together."

"Are you sure he wants to include me?"

"He said he'd pick you up. The way you are now, I can't see how you'd be much help."

"What way am I?"

"Mean and snotty and little. Thinking about your pride instead of Linn."

"Well, if you're right then I'm ashamed," I said. (I knew she was wrong.) "What time is he supposed to come by?"

"In about an hour."

"Snappy service. We ought to call on Uncle Candy more often. Hell, just the other day I had a flat tire."

"There's no point in our quarreling about it."

"Right you are. Anyway, he hasn't allowed us enough time for a really good one."

She shuffled her legs under the bedclothes. "It also doesn't seem a very auspicious time for one."

"Right again. I'll fix you a supper tray and get dressed, and by that time he ought to be here."

"I'm not hungry."

"You'd better eat something. It'll be good for your flu and good for your nerves."

"I couldn't keep it down. I really don't feel good."

167

"Sure?"

"Positive."

She picked up an issue of *Immaculate Homes* or whatever, plopped it on her lap and thumbed it open crossly.

"Whatever you say."

But when I was back in the kitchen I busied myself making a light meal for her, after first pouring another weak bourbon. Opened and watered and stirred a can of chicken noodle soup, sliced cheese and toasted a sandwich. After much rummaging I found a battered enameled tray and wiped it clean, laid out silver and the hasty food. It didn't look quite right, so I went into the living room and found a magazine with a colorful ad for mail order rosebushes. I clipped the photograph of an unbelievably fecund plant and slid it on the tray by the glass of skim milk. Going up the stairs I heard Katherine shift over in bed and click off the bedside lamp. She'd heard me coming. When I entered the room her face was turned away from me, half-buried in the pillow. I tiptoed over, grinning, and put the tray on the night stand, and as I went out I turned off the lamp on the dresser. The room was dark.

But it brightened again as I went back down the stairs. She had turned the light on and was sitting up to eat.

I had planned to change shirts and put on a tie, but decided the hell with it. My clothes were upstairs in the bedroom, and to return to change would lessen the drama of the quarrel. And it would embarrass Katherine. Anyway, I wasn't going to dignify Uncle Zeb with clean linen.

I strengthened my waning drink and carried it into the living room; sat on the sofa and sipped at it while waiting, staring vaguely at the corner of the ceiling.

He hadn't changed an ounce. It was the first time he'd visited our home and he looked about the room with an air of partly hidden condescension. He wasn't, of course, looking at the furnishings or the two paintings but at his estimate of my salary. And he was pleased that it wasn't what you'd call grand.

168

"Well, son," he said. "Looks like we've got a mite of trouble. Nothing to worry about, though. Could happen to anybody."

"Yes, but it's never easy."

"No. You're right there. It's never easy."

"Well, sir, sit down and let me fix you a drink."

"That sounds mighty good," he said, treating himself to the platform rocker. "I was beginning to get a little dry at the edges."

"What'll you have?"

"Oh, a tot of bourbon with about as much water as you can wring out of a turnip."

"Coming up."

Although I was beginning to feel slightly giddy—having not eaten—I carried my own glass back to the kitchen and made two drinks. Wrapped a paper napkin about Uncle Zeb's drink and handed it to him carefully before resuming my seat on the sofa. He took a first sip and gave me a beam of gratitude.

"Just what the doctor ordered," he said.

I smiled.

He leaned forward, digging his elbows into his knees, holding his glass loosely between them. "Now Katy has given me to understand that you-all haven't been informed of the charges."

"Who?" I said.

"Katy." He chuckled. "That's your wife's name, son."

My God: Katy. After a generation of my calling her Katherine.

"Oh."

"Now, the truth of the matter is, I don't think there is any real charge against your boy. If they wanted to be real sons of bitches, they might try to stick him with attempted robbery and maybe indecent exposure, but I don't think they want to do that. The only real trouble was that he wouldn't tell them his name, so they didn't know how to get in touch with you. If they could have got hold of you they wouldn't even have held him downtown."

"Good Lord," I said. "Robbery and indecent exposure? What in the world was Linn trying to do?"

Uncle Zeb giggled. It was a subterranean, gurgly, bog-water sort of giggle. "That's kind of hard to piece together," he said.

169

"You're going to have to get the whole story out of the boy when we get him home. The policemen found him up on top of an old stock feed warehouse out in the country here east of town."

"What was he doing?"

"Well." He giggled again; a nerve-racking noise. "Well, when they turned the light on him he was pissing off the roof. Pretty near showered down on one of our fine policemen."

"Good Lord."

"That's the indecent exposure charge," he said cheerfully. "But they're not really serious about it. Like I was telling you, they just put down something to hold him, waiting for identification."

"What about the robbery?"

"Well now, that's *his* story, not theirs. When they asked him what he was up to, he said he was attempting to break and enter. They couldn't hardly believe him. It'd be plain to anybody with the least grain of sense that there ain't no money in any kind of place like that. Any dope could figure that out, and from what I understand, your boy's a right smart lad. Takes after his daddy, I reckon."

"What was he after then, if not money?"

"Naturally the policemen asked him that too. And what he told them was that he was trying to steal some chicken feed."

"Steal what?"

He set his glass carefully on the end table and quite deliberately slapped his thigh. "Chicken feed. Can you beat that?"

"Good Lord."

"Chicken feed. Did you ever hear the beat?"

"What in the world?"

"That was my identical reaction. I was talking to Sergeant Gaffin over the phone, and I says, Well, Sarge, I don't see no way this case is ever going to be famous in the annals of crime. I don't believe it's the kind of case a great detective makes his reputation by solving. Course he agreed with me. He says, Well, you're right, Mr. Mackie, but you can see how we was up against it. —He meant, not knowing your boy's name or nothing."

170

"His name's Linn," I said. I was getting sick of *your boy.*

"Linn," he said, pondering. "That's not a family name, as I recall."

"Yes," I said. "My family."

"And I says, Sarge, it just don't sound like a very bloodthirsty crime. Matter of fact, I says, I believe you're going to be hard put to show how it was a criminal act at all. And he says, Mr. Mackie, you're right. —So that's where we stand. The police are willing to forget the whole thing if we'll go down and sign a few papers and pick up your boy. No reason to think it'll ever come to court."

"I'm glad it's nothing serious," I said. "But I can't understand it a bit. What in the world did Linn think he was doing?"

"Now let me ask you," Uncle Zeb said. "Do you have any notion at all what he was doing way out on that side of town?"

"He was staying overnight with some friends of his at a cabin at the foot of the mountain."

Uncle Zeb slapped his thigh again, rather more spontaneously this time and with evident self-satisfaction. "That's just how I'd got it figured," he said. "He's got out there with some of his buddies, you see, and the boys get to talking and going on and donkeying one another and pretty soon they get to daring one another and taking bets and egging each other on. You know how boys are. They start doing that and after a while it gets to the place where one of them can't back down. That makes him the man, you see. So then he's the one that's got to go ahead and do whatever foolish idle notion they all thought up. You mark my words, that's just exactly what took place."

"You're probably right." I had to agree with him, and, worse, I found myself beginning to like the old bastard again. "I remember how it was."

He picked up his drink and leaned back in the rocker. "Any man that's been a real boy will remember," he said. His voice became confidential, oozy: "I remember one time there was a bunch of us boys—Jack Starnes was one of them, you know the alderman here?—had got together one Friday. And we was just

171

going on. Pretty soon somebody says, Boys, I'd like to see the look on old Josh Joiner's face when he got up tomorrow morning and found his brand-new Columbia buggy in the top of that big old holly tree in his front yard. That was what started it, you see. So then we got to bullyragging one another, going round and round, till finally it lit on me. I'll be the one to take the wheels off and climb up and put them back on, I says, if you fellers'll do the rest of the work. I wasn't expecting nothing to happen, plain sure that nobody was taking me up on it. And then Jack Starnes, bless his heart, jumps up and says, Boys, we'll do it eleven tonight when the moon goes down. And we did. Did a full day's work from midnight on, and there wasn't one of us that didn't have to get up *awful* early in the morning and get to work farming. Worse, we didn't even get to hide and peep at old Josh when he saw his Columbia up there. We heard about it, though, how he went and got his shotgun and all."

I was almost over my ears in the folksiness, but I couldn't see how to stop it. "That's the way young people are, all right."

"I'll bet a pretty that's just how it was with your boy. Got to jollying and carrying on, and couldn't stop."

"I'm sure you're right," I said. "But hadn't we better go down and see about him? His good time has been over a long while now."

"I can see you're anxious," he said. "But there's nothing to be worried about now."

"I'd still like to see him."

"All right then," he said. "Course there's plenty of time yet. Wasn't it nine o'clock you said you'd meet your man Pape?" He rose readily from his chair.

Once more he had startled me. "Do you know Mr. Pape?"

"I know who he is," he said. "And I think he knows who I am. But we've never met. Come on, then. We'll take a short detour on the way down."

I got up, a bit unsteadily now, and we went out the door and down the walk and got into Uncle Zeb's car. It was a big black

172

Lincoln Continental. He went round and slid in behind the wheel, still talking.

He said, "I do believe I know a little bit more about Pape than he knows about me."

He started the car and we pulled away. Smooth and silent.

"How's that?"

"He's a bondsman, you know."

"Yes."

"He's also a bookmaker."

"I know that too."

"And among other things he's got him a little string of whores he makes some money off of."

"I didn't know that."

"Yes. I know a little something about him because I know a lot of fellers like him. He comes from down on Gimlet Street, has a foreign immigrant background. Gypsy, I bet a pretty. Course you got to admire him because he's come up a long way, done right well for himself, considering that to start with he didn't have a pot to piss in. But maybe he's beginning to get a little too big for his britches."

"What do you mean? How do you know so much about him?"

"Well, he's starting to edge a little bit into politics. Not so's you could tell it, not from reading the newspaper. But politics is my business, you see, and I make it a practice to know everything I can about my business, whatever it is."

"And you want to make sure he doesn't get too powerful."

Uncle Zeb gave me a pale sidelong glance, then returned his eyes to the road. He was taking a route that was unfamiliar to me until I realized that we were headed for the Gimlet Street section, the longer way around. I couldn't fathom his motives now. Was he preparing for some sort of object lesson?

"I wouldn't put it that way exactly," he said. "I never met the person face to face. I'd like to do that, to gauge him. Kind of feel him out, if you know what I mean . . . See, up here politics is kind of a family business. Not many people get into office that

173

ain't more or less born into office. But there's all kinds of other people that can make a difference, get the right kind of connections and all. May not seem to you like it would amount to much, but it's true." He gave a half sigh. "It's a complicated thing."

"I think I understand."

He turned his head, winked at me and drove on in silence.

We pulled off Flint onto Gimlet. I'd never been here at night and now I saw it with new eyes, though it was still the same place: beer parlors, greasy cafes, hot dog shops, shoeshine stands, secondhand stores. The open-air market at the lower end was closed, gates of two-by-fours and chicken wire enclosing the long benches. The weathered crumbling brick of the old buildings tingeing with blue, yellow, green, orange, as the neon signs flicked off and on. Rows of men in rolled shirt sleeves hunched over counters behind greasy windows. Sad diagonal lights that spelled BEER steadfastly. The sidewalk was crowded with milling idle people, farmers, soldiers, men in shirts with the names of their employers stitched on the backs, prostitutes.

"It ain't as pretty as some sections of town, is it?" Uncle Zeb asked.

"No," I said. "I'm afraid it's not very pretty."

"And yet you'd be surprised. Business is lively around here. A lot of money to be made in this section if a feller knows what he's about and keeps on his toes. But it takes a lot of maneuvering, and that's why you got to look out for these people. Because when they've come from around here they've been where it's a tough place and there's things they know that maybe not too many people know. It's a different kind of education from thinking about Latin and history."

We stopped for a light and on my side of the corner was a joint called the Champagne Club, small and dingy, with faded brown curtains pulled closed behind the omnipresent beer sign. The red leatherette door opened and a thin hatchet-faced girl came out, followed by a red-faced soldier who was obviously quite drunk. She had a head of amazing hair, dun blond, dry, frizzy, electric;

174

and she stood waiting for a moment until the soldier lurched against her. She made an angry face and said something I couldn't hear—Uncle Zeb was still talking—and gave the soldier a shove. When he pawed unsteadily at the air in front of her she slapped him sharply across the nose with a red clutch bag.

The light changed and we drove on.

". . . More fights and knifings on a Saturday night than you could shake a stick at," Uncle Zeb was saying. "But that's the way these people are. Manual labor jobs—they work hard, they want some hard excitement. They ain't going to be satisfied with sitting in the movies and holding hands. . . ."

We slid noiselessly past the darkened windows and the garish windows, past the men passing bottles in the alleys and the girls tugging at shrugging shoulders, past the rust-streaked cola signs and the mournful torn awnings, until we emerged from Gimlet and turned left into the town square.

When we passed the statue of Zebulon Johns I expected Uncle Zeb to take up the theme of Family again, but he didn't. "Where is it you're supposed to meet this Pape feller?" he asked.

"In the parking lot next to the jail."

It was a large square area on the right side of the jail and slightly downhill, no more interesting than an empty boxing ring, and surrounded by the kind of streetlamp that makes one's lips purple. There were more parked cars than I had expected and it took a minute to spot Mr. Pape. He was leaning against the pale Cadillac, which looked bluish in this odd light, carefully pulling at a cigar.

Uncle Zeb found a space and we got out and walked across.

"Good evening, Mr. Harper," Mr. Pape said.

"Hello," I said. We shook hands and I asked him if he'd been in to see Linn yet.

"No sir," he said. "I thought I'd wait till you arrived." He offered his hand to Uncle Zeb. "I don't believe we've met," he said.

"Oh, excuse me," I said. Because of Uncle Zeb's remarks I'd

forgotten that they'd never actually met. "Mr. Pape, this is my uncle, Mr. Mackie."

"Not Zeb Mackie, don't tell me," Mr. Pape said. They shook. "I've heard an awful lot of good things about you for an awful long time, Mr. Mackie. It's a real pleasure, sir." He seemed pleasurably surprised.

But Uncle Zeb didn't come on with his good-old-country-buddy routine. He spoke with a distant, almost cold, reserve. "Mr. Pape." And in shaking hands he gave a stiff jerk of his head which could almost be taken for a formal bow. "I've heard about you too, I believe."

The dark man was again surprised, but obviously not pleasurably this time. "Oh?"

"Heard you had some connection with the Sluder boys."

"Happens I do know the Sluders, represent them in one matter or another from time to time."

"People call you Oxie, don't they?" Uncle Zeb asked.

Now it was Mr. Pape's turn to become reserved. And wary. It seemed to me that I was watching the two men from outside, as through a department-store window, from another kind of space entirely; and that while I stood watching, maintaining my own position, they receded from one another, putting a rapid and hostile distance between themselves.

"It was a nickname I had. Seems to hang on with some people."

Uncle Zeb nodded. "Depending on the part of town?"

"Depending on how long they've known me."

I looked from one to the other, trying to puzzle it out, but my thoughts were interrupted.

What happened next was at first almost incomprehensible to me—and, in fact, I do not yet understand it. That is, I cannot know the causes and mechanics of the event. But it does take a shape in my mind, it does make itself at least credible. Even at the time it occurred it must have appealed to me as pattern, for by the time it was over I was laughing uncontrollably.

176

I heard behind me footsteps on the asphalt, footsteps quick and clumsy and skittery, as if someone were trying to charge fast and at the same time sneak up. When I turned to look I was accosted by the sight of someone in a bright blue-and-white rayon blazer coming toward us blurry, half-crouched. At first I took it to be a child, but when he stepped among us he straightened and I saw that it was an adolescent boy, very short, almost a midget. He had long smears of greasy blond hair and his reddened face was contorted into sharp savage lines.

"I knew by God I'd find you here," he shrieked. An amazing high-pitched sound: like metal shearing.

Mr. Pape dropped his cigar; ash dropped on his vest. "Arkie, you little—"

"Shut up," said the young man. "Shut your facehole, big shot."

He had been holding his hands in the pocket of his blazer and now he brought them out and in the right hand was a small-caliber pistol, an automatic. Even in his thin hands it didn't look very large.

Mr. Pape stepped forward, then back again. "Arkie—"

"I done told you," the young man said. "Anyway, it ain't you. It's him." He turned and pointed the pistol at Uncle Zeb. "It's this goddam pervert. Think you're something, huh? All dressed up and white-headed. But you ain't nothing but a creepy old pervert that can't do nothing but bust up on women." He giggled crazily. "Not no more you don't, you silly old bastard."

He steadied the pistol with his left hand and fired.

Bang.

Mr. Pape was shouting. "Arkie, you crazy fucker, the cops will—"

"Fuck them!" he shouted. "Fuck the law, I'm going down to ARKANSAS!"

And with this mystifying prophecy he flung away the pistol and scuttled off, disappearing among the parked cars like a spider going down into its nest.

The bullet had struck Uncle Zeb. He trembled and then went

177

backward with short palsied steps like dance steps. When his hip struck the sharp tail fin of the Cadillac his feet went out from under him and he slid down, leaning against the tire. He slid down hard. His eyes were bright and watery and he breathed hoarse and deep.

Mr. Pape and I ran to him.

"God damn it," he said. His teeth were clenched hard.

I pulled back his jacket, and the whole left side of his shirt front was resplendent with blood. I looked anxiously, trying to find the wound.

"God damn it," he said again.

Finally I located it. A hole about the size of a dime, pouring blood, and jagged with shreds of bone. The bullet had gone high, had broken his collarbone. That was all. I let go his jacket and sat myself down on the pavement. My breathing stopped shuddering. It was then that I began laughing and laughing.

Because it wasn't serious. It must have been deliciously painful, but it wasn't serious. It was just something he could tell later to his nieces and nephews and grandchildren. A story. He could sit on the front porch on a warm summer evening and tell the younger generation exactly what had happened.

Assuming of course that they'll listen to him.